TALES
FROM
TRINITY

TALES
FROM
TRINITY

A Novel by
Jim Bornzin

iUniverse, Inc.
Bloomington

TALES FROM TRINITY

iUniverse books may be ordered through booksellers or by contacting:

iUniverse
1663 Liberty Drive
Bloomington, IN 47403
www.iuniverse.com
1-800-Authors (1-800-288-4677)

ISBN: 978-1-4759-6597-1 (sc)
ISBN: 978-1-4759-6598-8 (ebk)

Library of Congress Control Number: 2012923126

Printed in the United States of America

iUniverse rev. date: 01/25/2013

ACKNOWLEDGEMENTS

The tales from Trinity are fiction, though some have roots in the author's experiences as a Lutheran parish pastor. The characters in these stories are also fiction. No similarity to church members past or present is intended.

The author is grateful to Linda Wold, Sharon Larcom, and other friends who encouraged the attempt at a second book about the fictitious Trinity Lutheran, and deeply indebted to the following friends who read the early manuscript and made suggestions for improvement: Pastor Paul Doellinger, Chris Brown, and my sister-in-law Deborah Bornzin. Your significant contributions to the quality of this novel cannot be overstated. Editors at iUniverse also provided suggestions which greatly enhanced development of the characters and stories. Any shortcomings are the responsibility of the author.

Appreciation is also due my friends in the Writers Club of Silverton who listened patiently to my initial efforts.

My wife and sons have encouraged my adventure in writing, and to them I say, "I love you and thank you for all you have done for me and meant to me through the years."

INTRODUCTION

What if Your blessings come through raindrops?
What if Your healing comes through tears?
What if a thousand sleepless nights
Are what it takes to know You're near?
And what if the trials of this life
The rain, the storms, the hardest nights,
Are Your mercies in disguise?

From the song "Blessings" by Laura Story

Life is not always what it seems. Sometimes, what seems like the end is really a new beginning. Sometimes, God uses rain to make the flowers bloom, and sometimes God uses tears to wash away the old and usher in the new. Sleepless nights may feel like the absence of God; yet all the while, God is near and working miracles.

These are the *Tales from Trinity:* stories of raindrops and sunshine, tears and laughter, sleepless nights, heartache and sorrows, which, when woven together by God, helped create a "real family" for Mike Greenwood, Kathy Stiletto, Reiner and Tillie Holtz, and others in Weston. The story of Trinity Lutheran is not just Pastor Paul Walker's story, but the story of God's people in Weston, Indiana. Some are members of Paul's church and family; some are not. Some are happy; some are not. And what if the trials of this life, the rain, the storms, the hardest nights, are God's mercies in disguise?

TABLE OF CONTENTS

PART 1

PART 2

PART 3

PART 1

1

Fred Wilson arrived at the church on a hot, sunny, Saturday afternoon in July, fifteen minutes before the meeting was to begin. Since the congregation was between pastors, he was tempted to park in the space marked *PASTOR*, but his conscience wouldn't let him. He loved Trinity Lutheran's old brick building, its cross and steeple, though it seemed to him the cross was leaning slightly; or maybe it was just the angle at which he viewed it from the parking lot. Fred jiggled the key in the old church door and it finally opened. From the landing, he headed down to the church basement.

As chairman of the Call Committee, he felt responsible for every detail of the call process. He had learned years ago that Lutheran pastors are *called,* not *hired*, as in the business world, indicating that, in an important way, God is involved.

Fred knew that the search for a new pastor would have a profound impact on the church's future. The committee had been elected by the congregation and was chosen to represent various groups within the church: three women, three men, one retired member, one high-school youth, etc. Fred was a dentist by profession, well-respected in town and well-loved by many in the congregation. His thick, wavy hair had turned pre-maturely gray, making him appear somewhat older than his forty-six years. Bright blue eyes and a warm, radiant smile invited trust; and Fred had proven trustworthy to everyone who knew him. In past years he had served several terms on the congregation council, one term as the president.

The basement fellowship hall of the old church had very small windows and was rather dark. At least it was cooler in the basement than it was outside. Fred was glad he wasn't wearing a tie and coat. Informal attire was acceptable in this heat. He turned on the overhead fluorescent lights, began arranging the tables in a U, and placed folding chairs around the tables. Six chairs were for members of the committee and two chairs at the head table for the pastor and his wife. Louise Downing had promised to bring refreshments and serve coffee. Fred was hopeful that Pastor Paul Walker, their second candidate, would be a perfect match for Trinity.

Two weeks ago, the committee had met with Pastor Ryan Armbruster, a business-like clergyman in his early fifties. Ryan had interviewed well, seemed confident, though not overly enthusiastic about their church in an older part of Weston, Indiana. He was currently serving as the Associate Pastor of a large suburban church near Indianapolis. Rick Rousch, the banker on the Call Committee, had taken a liking to Ryan. Fred supposed it was because of Ryan's attention to details, church organization, and the finances of the congregation. Liz Sterling, a realtor, also seemed impressed with Ryan. But as Fred pondered the reaction of the other committee members, he felt they were less enthusiastic.

Fred Schmidt, one of Trinity's retired members and a faithful usher, came down the basement steps into the fellowship hall. Fred wore a sport shirt and jeans, sported a handle-bar mustache, and had a knack for putting people at ease. "Hey, Fred!" he hollered.

"Hey, yourself, Fred!" the chairman responded. "How are you today?"

"Mighty fine!" Schmidt replied. "Maybe we should play Dr. Seuss! I'll be Fred One and you can be Fred Two!"

The chairman chuckled, "No way! I'm the chairman. I should be Fred One! You're Fred Two!"

By the time Fred Schmidt reached the bottom of the steps, the three women on the committee came through the parking lot door together. They had met outside and agreed to help carry things downstairs. Louise was carrying two large carafes of coffee that she had just finished brewing at home. Liz, the real estate agent, and Traci Malsberger, a high-school student and cheerleader at Weston High, were carrying trays of brownies and cookies still warm from the oven.

"Hi! Mr. Wilson! Hi! Mr. Schmidt!" Traci greeted the older men as she placed the brownies on the table. Liz set down the tray of cookies, straightened her skirt, and took her seat. The smell of fresh baked brownies wafted through the room.

A few minutes later Rick Rousch arrived and took his seat next to Traci. Rick was dressed for the meeting in his suit and tie, which he was accustomed to wearing at the bank no matter what the weather. Glancing at his Armani titanium watch, he noted to himself that he was punctual as usual, and it was time for the meeting to start. "Did everyone read the pastoral profile for the new candidate?" he asked, not wanting to waste any precious time with small talk. Members began fumbling with their notebooks and folders with profiles and notes. "The guy's only been ordained for six years," Rick continued.

"Why don't we begin with a prayer?" Fred Wilson suggested, just slightly annoyed that Rick was in such a hurry to begin. "Heavenly Father, we ask your blessing on our interview today. Be with us and with our next candidate as we become acquainted with him and his wife. Grant Pastor Paul and Cheri a safe trip from Wisconsin, and may your Holy Spirit guide us in our conversation and search for a new pastor. Amen."

Fred continued, "Louise, I want to thank you for providing the coffee and refreshments today. I hope you've all had time to review the pastoral profile for Paul Walker who should be arriving in about thirty minutes. Let's take a few minutes to look over the profile and discuss any questions you may have before the interview. I felt our meeting with Pastor Ryan went well a couple of weeks ago, so I hope you'll be prepared with your interview questions again this week. Remember to keep the questions open-ended, so the candidate can reply with more than just a yes or no."

A lively discussion followed based on the information provided by Pastor Walker. Rick pointed out the fact that Paul was quite a bit younger than Ryan Armbruster, and that Paul had been pastor at only one church. Liz

Sterling said quite frankly she was more impressed with Pastor Ryan's profile than Paul Walker's.

Suddenly a voice was heard from up the stairs. "Hello! Anyone here?" It was the candidate, Pastor Paul Walker.

"Yes! Hello! We're down here in the fellowship hall!" Fred hollered back.

Paul and his wife, Cheri, came down the stairs and began shaking hands with members of the call committee. Paul was neatly attired in khakis and a light blue long-sleeve shirt. Cheri was in slacks and a summer blouse, light pink with white flowers and a ruffled front. Both seemed energetic considering the long drive from Twin Lakes, Wisconsin. Cheri's smile lit up the room, and her dimples were the feature Paul had first fallen in love with many years ago.

Fred Wilson invited Paul and Cheri to sit at the head table, introduced the members of the committee, and then welcomed Paul and Cheri to Trinity. A series of lively questions and answers followed. Paul talked enthusiastically about his ministry in Twin Lakes; and Cheri spoke about their two sons, Chip and Randy. Paul asked committee members to describe their church's neighborhood and the mission of the congregation. Soon it was time for a break. After refreshments, Cheri was given a tour of Weston by Mrs. Rousch and Mrs. Wilson, the wives of the committee members. The committee resumed its discussion with Paul who seemed eager to serve an inner-city congregation.

That evening, Paul and Cheri were invited to spend the night in the home of Stan and Beth Malsberger, whose daughter Traci, was on the committee. Beth prepared a delicious home-cooked dinner of baked ham, mashed potatoes and peas. Stan was an electrical contractor and chairman of the Building and Property Committee, and it was evident he knew every nook and cranny of the building. "It's an old church, but we love it! Built in 1948, right after the war, she requires a lot of maintenance, but I don't mind. Kind of enjoy it actually." Traci eventually tired of the grown-ups' conversation and went upstairs to her bedroom.

On Sunday morning, Cheri and Paul sat near the front of the church with the Malsbergers. The Call Committee had asked Paul to preach the sermon. A well-attended social hour followed worship. The Walkers enjoyed meeting everyone, and they were delighted with the wonderful reception they received. Sunday afternoon they drove home to Wisconsin, talking excitedly for five hours straight about the interview and the possibility of living in Weston, Indiana, about seventy miles south of Chicago.

*   *   *

A week later, the call committee met after worship to discuss the two candidates. Traci, bubbling with teenage excitement, could hardly contain herself. "I really like Pastor Paul. He's younger than Pastor Ryan, and he'll relate better to the youth in our church. His wife Cheri is really nice too! She even helped my mom do the dishes after dinner!"

Fred Schmidt responded next. "He may be young, but I think he related well to us retired folks also. Everyone I've talked to since last Sunday seems really excited about the Walkers."

Rick decided it was time to put in a word for Ryan Armbruster. "I think this church needs a pastor with more experience. We're a small congregation; and we need someone who's good at administration as well as preaching and youth work. If we consider all the aspects of pastoral leadership, I think our choice will have to be Pastor Ryan."

"Pastor Ryan certainly has more experience, but I think a young pastor will help draw more young people to our church," Louise Downing responded. "Our former pastor, had a lot of experience too, and our older members loved him, but we need to start bringing in young families."

"I agree that our older members loved Pastor Bjornstad," commented Fred Schmidt, "but he was rather old-fashioned, and he certainly didn't generate enthusiasm. I liked Pastor Walker's energy and openness and sense of humor. I think he would be a great match for us right now."

"How about you, Liz?" Fred Wilson asked. "You've been quiet so far."

Liz was furious inside but smiled politely. "Oh, I'm willing to go along with the rest of the committee. Whatever the rest of you think would be best."

Liz Sterling could hardly believe what was happening! She was still upset that she hadn't been chosen as chair of this committee. She was the principal broker for Weston Realty, with over a million dollars in sales the past five years, and the president of the Association of Northern Indiana Realtors. These naïve dreamers had chosen Fred Wilson as their chairman, and now they were all a-twitter over the young pastor from Wisconsin! Rick Rousch had made it clearly evident why Pastor Armbruster was the superior candidate. It appeared, however, that the choice of Trinity's pastor, and perhaps the future of Trinity, was in the hands of an excitable teenager, a housewife, and an old retired guy. She could hardly wait to hear what Fred Wilson's opinion would be.

"How about you, Mr. Chairman?" Liz smiled and stared at Fred.

Fred paused and looked around at the other members. Four were smiling; only Rick was not. "I think we've been blessed with two very well-qualified candidates. Each of them is a good pastor. I think we need to look at the issue of 'fit.' Which candidate's qualifications best fit our mission here in Weston, and the needs of our members, and the needs of this community? What I observed at the Sunday receptions after worship, the way each candidate interacted with our members, leads me to believe that Pastor Paul Walker would be a better fit for Trinity."

Fred waited again for any response. Rick spoke once more. "I hear what you're saying; and there may be some merit to it. I know my preference for Pastor Ryan is based on my personal feelings about him and my respect for his experience and his priorities. However, I don't know if the rest of you picked up on this, but I felt Ryan himself wasn't too excited about coming here . . . . So maybe Paul Walker would work out better. I'm willing to recommend him if that's how the rest of you feel."

Liz was still seething, and still smiling. The wishy-washy banker had 'caved.'"

"Are you ready then, to vote on a candidate?" chairman Wilson asked the committee.

"I move that we recommend Pastor Paul Walker to the council and the congregation, to be the next pastor here at Trinity Lutheran Church," Fred Schmidt declared.

"All in favor, say Aye," Fred Wilson replied.

"Aye," they all responded.

"Then it's unanimous," Fred concluded. "We'll make our recommendation to the council, and they'll prepare a *Letter of Call* to Pastor Walker for the congregational meeting two weeks from tomorrow. If I remember correctly, the call requires a two-thirds vote of the congregation. I'll call the council president, Bill Trogdon, tonight. He told me he was anxious to hear our decision."

"Do you anticipate any problems from the council or the congregational meeting?" Rick asked.

"The congregation council will receive our recommendation on Monday night. I don't expect any problems there. I'm sure they have the salary figures, health insurance, pension contribution, and benefits prepared to add to the Letter of Call. Based on what we saw from the congregation members, I can't imagine they'll do anything but support our recommendation."

"I'm excited!" Traci added. "I can't wait to tell my friends. Do you think Pastor Walker will accept the call?" she asked.

"I certainly hope so," Fred replied.

2

Cheri and Paul were excited about the call to Weston. Paul drafted an enthusiastic letter of acceptance and read it to Cheri. "Let's get it in the mail," she responded. Neither of them had ever lived in Indiana, and they would actually be a little closer to Paul's parents who were living in Des Moines. The first thing they would have to do is find a house. After announcing to their congregation in Twin Lakes, Wisconsin, that Paul had accepted a new call to Trinity in Weston, they put their house on the market and began looking for a new home in Weston.

It was a warm August morning when they dropped the boys off at a friend's and drove to Indiana. They had arranged to meet Liz Sterling at her Weston Realty office at two o'clock that afternoon. Since Liz was a realtor and had served on the call committee, it seemed only natural to ask if she would help them with their house hunting. Liz was well-prepared when they arrived, and they spent the next several hours driving around town looking at homes. At five o'clock she took them back to their motel and reminded them that all expenses would be reimbursed by Trinity. "See you bright and early in the morning!" she said as they climbed out of her car. She still had four more listings she wanted them to see.

Their room was clean and cool; the air-conditioner hummed noisily. Paul flopped on the king-size bed. "That was an interesting afternoon!" Paul sighed. "Why don't you clean up first? I'll take a shower when you're done."

"Oh yeah, this is gonna feel good!" Cheri replied as she headed for the bathroom. After a shower and change of clothes, Paul and Cheri walked to the restaurant next to the motel for dinner.

"What did you think of the homes we saw today?" Cheri asked as they opened the menus.

"A couple of them were real 'fixer-uppers' as they say. But there were two newer homes that I thought had possibilities," Paul reflected as he browsed the menu.

"I really liked that second house," Cheri said, "the one with the swing set in the back yard. The boys would love that!"

"Yeah, I liked that one too. I liked the three bedrooms. One could be a study/office for either or both of us," Paul replied.

"And . . . it was only five blocks from the elementary school," Cheri added.

After placing their order, Paul looked at Cheri and decided to ask a question about something that had been bothering him. "So . . . what did you think of Liz?"

Cheri thought for a moment, wondering why Paul was asking, "I thought she was very helpful and very professional. Why?"

"Did you notice that whenever I asked her a question about a house, or a certain feature, she looked away from me and gave me a curt reply? Maybe I'm just imagining it, but I felt like I was being talked down to or scolded."

"Really? To be honest, no, I hadn't noticed. Are you sure you aren't just being paranoid?"

"Well, I suppose I could be. But something about her makes me uncomfortable."

"Oh, Paul, you are so sensitive; and you just want everyone to like you. But . . . I'll tell you what.

Tomorrow, I'll watch when she talks to you and see if maybe . . . just maybe . . . you're right."

"Thanks, honey. It's probably nothing to worry about."

"Or maybe . . ." Cheri leaned forward and whispered, "She's out to GET YOU!" They both burst into laughter as the waitress came with their dinner.

Back in her office Liz Sterling was reflecting on the tour with the Walkers. She had to admit Cheri seemed nice enough, but Paul . . . ? As they walked through the homes, Liz noticed that Paul seemed anxious, and at times, very critical of what he saw. She noticed that Paul picked at his nails and sometimes tore them off at the tip of his finger. It reminded her of the interview at which she actually saw him biting his fingernail. *What a disgusting habit! How could this man have been called as our pastor? Well, one more day should do it. They seemed really excited about the three bedroom bungalow. At least I'll get a commission out of all this.*

A few weeks later papers were signed and the deal was closed. Much to Paul and Cheri's relief, their house in Twin Lakes also sold quickly. In late September the moving van loaded their belongings and the Walkers began a new adventure in Weston, Indiana.

The problems of an inner city church in an older neighborhood would test his faith and challenge his pastoral abilities. Within a month Paul fell in love with the old structure of Trinity Lutheran with its brick walls, stained glass windows, and tall steeple. Members told him that in years past, there was a light in the cross on top of the steeple which could be seen from all over Weston. The bell in the bell tower had been cast in Holland and was rung by the ushers, briefly on Sunday mornings, ten minutes before worship. A large rope dangled through a hole from the tower into a small closet which was kept locked. The story was told that before it was locked, children used to hide in the closet; and when no adults were around, they would pull on the rope and toll the bell. Then they would dash from the closet into the sanctuary and act innocent!

Chip and Randy, their sons, seemed happy with the move as well. They adjusted quickly to their new school and began making new friends. Meanwhile, Paul was busy getting acquainted with members and the community. Fred Schmidt, from the Call Committee, became a respected and trusted friend almost immediately. Fred would call the office and ask the pastor if he had any plans for lunch, and out they would go to a local restaurant. There they talked about the church and their families. "I really hope you'll like Weston and stay with us for a long time," Fred told him on their first visit. It appeared Fred's only agenda was to support his pastor.

The parish secretary, Carol Von Schoyck, was easy to work with. She paid attention to detail, always seemed to be in a good mood, and made people feel very welcome when they came into the office. Most of the leaders and council members were solid people also. Bill Trogdon was the president. Rick Rousch did an excellent job as treasurer. Stan Malsberger irritated Paul at times, being a little too protective of the church building and property, constantly worried about liability, but Paul appreciated his concerns.

The only person who made Paul uncomfortable was Liz Sterling, the realtor. She came to church with her husband, Phillip Sterling, a general contractor with his own business, Sterling Homes. Paul made a get-acquainted visit at their home and found Phillip quite affable, but Liz did little to put him at ease. He simply couldn't figure out what was troubling her.

Everyone in Weston seemed to know something about Trinity Lutheran Church. People referred to it as the church with the steeple at the corner of 16th and Oak. Folks often reminisced about Doc Anderson, family physician, school board member, and leader in Kiwanis. He was a generous contributor to every local fund raiser. His parents were charter members of Trinity in 1912, and Doc Anderson was the single largest donor for the new church built in 1948. Doc had passed away in 1963.

People also talked about Pastor Bjornstad, Paul's predecessor, who served Trinity for fifteen years. Pastor Bjornstad liked to hang out at the local restaurants and coffee shops, shooting the breeze with anyone who had time to visit. He finally retired, and he and his wife moved to Florida. Some of the older members told Paul they missed him, but a few families confided that, in their opinion, it was time for him to retire. Paul couldn't imagine retiring. There was so much work to be done.

3

Paul Walker was now in his fourth year at Trinity Lutheran. His wife Cheri had found a challenging position as office manager at Etheridge, Juarez, Fuscio, and Barkley, a highly-regarded law firm in Weston. Paul respected her desire to work professionally. Together they worked out their parental responsibilities and schedules. He and Cheri took turns coming home at 3 p.m. to welcome the boys home from school.

Paul's work patterns were well-established: office work in the morning, out visiting members or out in the community in the afternoons. This morning he arrived at the usual time, parked in his usual space, looked up at the steeple as he always did, and said a quick prayer as he walked to the door of the church. He put his key in the lock and turned to see his secretary, Carol, pulling into the parking lot. The lock wouldn't turn. He jiggled the key and pulled on the door and the lock finally opened. As fussy as Stan Malsberger was about a lot of things, Paul couldn't understand why he never fixed this lock.

Paul held the door for Carol and they went up the stairs to the office. The neighborhood was changing and so was the church. Paul had grown up in rural Iowa where it seemed to him as a child that nothing ever changed. In college he began to feel called to ministry and dreamed of serving an "inner city" church with the challenges and excitement that stir a young man's idealism. He pictured himself as a minister working with inner city teens and gangs. However, now that he was in the urban environment and had a family, urban ministry wasn't nearly as glamorous as he had dreamed it would be. The intercom buzzed, interrupting Paul's thoughts.

"It's Darrel Thomas on line 1," his secretary Carol announced.

Paul picked up the phone, "Good morning, Darrel."

"Good morning, Pastor Paul. I just thought I would call to give you a heads up about my report to the council next week. Have you looked at the cross on top of the steeple recently?"

"Well, Darrel, I see it every day, but I haven't really studied it for a while. What's wrong?"

"It's leaning."

"It's always had a slight lean, at least as long as I've been here. Is there something new?"

"I guess Stan Malsberger has been worried about the cross, so he asked me to look into the problem and report to the Building and Property Committee. Yesterday I climbed up into the steeple and guess what I saw?"

"A pigeon's nest?"

Darrel laughed. "Yeah . . . two or three old nests . . . but what fascinated me were two horizontal cross beams inside the steeple that make an X which holds up the cross. They seem pretty secure. But around the top of the steeple, where the cross pokes through, the wood is rotting. That's why it's leaning. And I may be seeing things, but I think it's leaning way more than it used to. I agree with Stan that a really strong wind could bring it down."

"Whoa! That could be a catastrophe!" Paul replied.

"Right! There's no telling how much damage would be done if it toppled and fell."

"You're right, Darrel. Can you get an estimate on what it would cost to repair the steeple or replace the cross?" asked Paul.

"I've looked into it and plan to make a report to the council next week, Pastor."

"I suppose it will cost a fortune."

"Just a small fortune," Darrel replied, "but I really feel we need to do something."

"I agree, and I'm pretty sure the council will too. I don't know where the money will come from, but as I tell others, we've got to trust in God." As he hung up the phone Paul again wondered, *What next?*

Carol, the parish secretary stood in the door, "Sorry to bother you, Pastor, but I saw the light go out on line 1, and I wanted to inform you, the water won't stop running in the women's bathroom."

"In the toilet or the sink?" Paul sighed, unable to hide his frustration with the nuts and bolts of everyday ministry. *I love this old church, but the maintenance never ends!*

"In the toilet," Carol replied.

"Did you check the float and the valve?"

"My husband always does that at home," Carol said imploringly.

"I'll go take a look," Paul sighed again as he rose from the desk.

*   *   *

At the council meeting on Monday night, Darrel gave his report on the cross. Everyone agreed something should be done as soon as possible. "We won't really know how extensive the damage is until we get the cross down," he reported. "I've got a guy coming on Friday with a crane. He says he can put a loop around the cross to hold it while we unbolt it from the cross beams underneath. At a hundred and twenty-five dollars an hour I hope it doesn't take too long to get it down."

15

That Friday, Pastor Paul Walker was sitting in his office and revising his sermon when the crane arrived. Paul was astounded at the length of the boom. As he made his way to the parking lot he noticed Darrel standing near the front steps talking with the crane operator. Paul joined the conversation. In a matter of minutes the crane was being extended, a large steel cable loop at the end. The skilled operator lassoed the cross and pulled the cable taught. Darrel climbed the ladder inside the steeple and began unbolting the bottom of the cross. When he returned to the front of the church, he reported that although the cross was made of sheet metal, it had a wooden core, about 8"x12" which extended from the base up inside the sheet metal cross, and the wooden core was soft and rotted also.

A few moments later the crane was lifting the cross free of the steeple as a handful of neighbors gathered to watch on the sidewalk across the street. The cross was carefully lowered to the street, and the small crowd clapped and cheered! The cable was removed, and Darrel, Paul, and several neighbors dragged the cross into the parking lot. It was a lot bigger and heavier than it had appeared when seventy feet atop the steeple.

"Pastor, we've got a problem, and I don't know why I didn't think of it before," Darrel spoke with a pleading expression on his face.

"What's the matter?" asked Paul, "We got it down, didn't we?"

"Yea, but the crane operator just asked me how we are going to cover the hole at the top of the steeple. If it rains, we'll have water all over the place."

"Well, we need to find something to cover the hole, like a piece of plastic, or a box."

"A sheet of plastic would blow off unless we strap it down somehow."

"Hang on Darrel, I'll see what I can find." Paul made his way to the office, took a quick look around and then headed to the basement. The door to the janitor's closet was ajar; Paul looked in and turned on the light. There was the answer to their problem. A large green 30 gallon plastic garbage can sat empty in the corner. That should just fit over the top of the steeple, Paul thought as he carried it upstairs.

The crane operator laughed as he saw the pastor approaching. He stepped into the bucket of the crane with the garbage can in hand, and using the remote control began the ascent. Everyone watched in awe as he stopped level with the top of the steeple. He turned the garbage can upside down and fit it snugly over the steeple top. Looking down at the crowd below, he gave a thumbs up sign. "Mission accomplished!" shouted Paul. The neighbors clapped and cheered again.

As the crane pulled away from the church and the crowd dispersed, Darrel and Paul stood looking at the old cross. The metal seams were rusted, several fluorescent bulbs from inside were broken, and the plexiglass through which the light shone was badly cracked. "I doubt that it's worth repairing," sighed Darrel.

"I'll bet it was quite a sight when it was new," Paul added. "Older members have always been very proud of that lighted cross, but I haven't seen it lit since I've been pastor here."

"No, the lights gave out years ago, and it was just too costly to bring a crane in to change the bulbs." Darrel sighed. "So what do we do now?"

"Why don't we get a committee of interested members together to see how a new cross might be made and how it might be lit with lights from below? It's going to take a lot of research and calling around to various companies. Darrel, are you willing to head that up?"

"Sure, pastor, I'll get to work on it. Maybe someone from the Memorial Committee would like to help. They're the only ones with funds available."

"You've got that right," Paul replied with a smile.

On Sunday morning all the members were talking about the old cross and how nice it would be to have a new one all lit up again! Then on Wednesday, everyone was shocked to see a photo of Trinity Lutheran at

Jim Bornzin

the bottom of the front page of the local *Weston Herald*. The caption read, **"Church of the Holy Garbage Can! Local church replaces cross with plastic garbage pail."**

* * *

Darrel Thomas was one of the first to call the Trinity office on Thursday morning. "Did you see the picture in yesterday's paper, Pastor?"

"Yes, Darrel. I guess all we can do is laugh."

"Along with the rest of the city," Darrel added. "I just wanted you to know, I'll get to work on getting the new cross up there as quickly as possible."

"Don't worry about it. I know these things take time. Maybe I can call the *Herald* and give them the complete story. Might even provide us another outreach opportunity."

"You may be right, Pastor. There are a lot of old-timers in this town who remember when the church was new and the cross was lit at night. They'd love to see it lit again."

"Do what you can, Darrel, and thanks for calling."

A couple of months later, just before Thanksgiving, the Steeple Committee (as they called themselves) reported their findings to the congregation council. Darrel explained the proposal. "First, the top of the steeple will be refinished, removing rotted boards at the top. A new 'cap' will be securely nailed in place which will be tapered at the same angle as the steeple. It will be square at the base and have a rectangular opening at the top through which the new cross will be lowered. The entire steeple will be re-shingled, and spotlights installed at the base. Second, we found a company that proposed a fiberglass cross which will be painted with several coats of high gloss enamel, like a shiny new white car. The advantage of fiberglass is that it is light, durable, weatherproof, and will flex slightly in strong winds. Near the base of the cross will be a small flared section which will fit exactly over the steeple 'cap' to prevent any rain or snow from seeping into the steeple."

"And how much is this project going to cost?" Rick Rousch, the treasurer, asked.

"I've spoken with the pastor, and I know there's nothing extra in the annual budget. We do have several thousand that the Memorial Fund Committee is willing to put toward the new cross."

"That doesn't exactly answer my question," the treasurer spoke again.

"Well, the total cost is going to be about four or five thousand dollars," Darrel admitted.

Bill Trogdon, the council president, suggested a *Steeple and Cross* fund appeal, asking the congregation for one-time donations. The council members agreed, and decided that Memorial Funds would be used as an incentive, matching special donations, dollar for dollar.

*   *   *

By March, the funds had been raised and a new cross had been fabricated. The weather, however, was not cooperating, and the council knew the new cross could not be installed until May. Members were so used to the green garbage can on top of the steeple that no one even commented on it any longer. Occasionally, a visitor to the church would ask about the strange sight, and they would be told the story of the old leaning cross and the plans for the new one.

As spring arrived, Darrel and his buddies finally got the new 'cap' block installed and ready for the new cross. It was decided that the second Sunday of Easter would be an appropriate day to celebrate the new cross and its installation. The cross was delivered on the Monday afternoon following Easter Sunday; Darrel had asked the pastor to call him at work when it arrived. He came rushing to the church just as the delivery truck was pulling away. Paul was standing in the parking lot, amazed again at its size.

"Pastor, we've got another problem. I've got the crane coming tomorrow morning, but I don't think we can get the cross inside the church tonight.

It's just too big!" They measured the cross beam at just over nine feet, too wide to fit through the church doors.

"I don't know, Darrel. I hate to leave it out here in the parking lot overnight, but it's too big to move." The two of them looked around to see if there was something on the building to which they could rope or chain the large cross. Not finding any way to secure it, Pastor Paul looked at Darrel, then looked up to the sky and said, "Let us pray. Dear Lord, once again we find ourselves hopeless and at your mercy. You obviously see our predicament. Could we possibly trouble you to keep an eye on the cross tonight? We may not sleep well, but we are going to put our trust in you. The crane is coming tomorrow. Please keep this cross safe. I hope we're not asking too much. Amen."

"Amen," echoed Darrel.

The next morning Paul was relieved to see the shiny white cross still lying in the parking lot where they had left it the night before. Thankfully, no graffiti had been painted on it. Darrel arrived soon after and waited in the pastor's office. When the crane arrived, a small group of members and neighbors gathered again across the street to watch. This time the crane raised both the crane operator in the basket, and the new cross by means of the cable loop. The operator guided the cross over the top of the steeple as Darrel again climbed up inside the steeple to fasten the cross to the X beams. The crane operator leaned over the steeple and removed the garbage can.

He gave the base of the cross a slight push to align it with the rectangular hole. "Ready?" he hollered. "Ready!" Darrel yelled from inside the steeple. The cable began to lower the cross into the steeple until it rested firmly on the X beams inside. Darrel quickly fastened the bolts into place to secure the base of the cross. The slight flare or flange about three feet up fit snugly over the top of the cap block. Perfect! "Base is secure!" Darrel hollered from inside the steeple.

The crane operator unhooked the cable loop from the cross and the crowd below began cheering. Trinity's new cross was on top of the steeple. Gone, but never-to-be-forgotten, was the green garbage can.

That evening, Darrel and his wife Francine, and the members of the Steeple Committee, together with the Memorial Committee, Stan Malsberger and his family, the Building and Property Committee, and the council members, all gathered in front of the church. Pastor Paul and Cheri, with sons Chip and Randy, stood there too, waiting for Darrel to set the timer on the new lights at the base of the steeple. The lights were pointed upwards to illuminate both the steeple and the cross. The members held their breath as they waited for the new lights to come on. They waited. They waited. Was something wrong with the lights?

Suddenly the steeple and cross were lit! Everyone applauded and cheered. The bright beacon of Trinity Lutheran shone once again over the city of Weston, and for a brief moment in time, all seemed right with the world.

4

Brian Holloway was a junior at Weston High School

when he began working part-time as the custodian for Trinity Lutheran. He was planning to attend Purdue University when he graduated, and he wanted to become a veterinarian. Sadly, his dreams were never fulfilled.

It was late one August evening when Paul got the phone call to come to the church right away. Brian's father sounded desperate. "I've called 9-1-1. They're sending an ambulance and the police." Paul raced to the church. *Something must have happened to Brian . . . ambulance . . . police?* The young custodian, Brian Holloway, was cleaning the church on Friday night when he apparently found someone who had broken into the church. Unfortunately, the intruder had a knife; and when Brian tried to stop him from getting away, he stabbed Brian several times. When Brian's father came to the church looking for his son, he found him dead in a pool of blood at the bottom of the stairs inside. It was the most horrible night for all of them, for Bob and Marge Holloway, for Brian's little sister Sarah, and for Pastor Paul and Cheri. Paul accompanied the Holloways to the hospital where the agony of grief was poured out over Brian's lifeless body. Then he returned home to share the horrible news with Cheri.

In the days that followed, Paul dealt with the shock and grief and fear and anger of the entire community. Funeral plans were made for Brian's memorial. Police officers from the homicide division were often at the church, talking with Paul, combing the building and neighborhood for clues about what happened and trying to find the killer.

The memorial service was a wonderful tribute to Brian. The vet, for whom Brian also worked part-time, talked about Brian's love for animals and his excellent work ethic. Brian's best friend, Michael Greenwood, talked about their friendship and Brian's sense of humor. And Brian's sister, Sarah, shared her love for her brother in a way that brought tears to everyone's eyes. It was an emotional release for everyone, but by no means was there any sense of closure. It took months to find the church intruder, and nearly a year before Brian's killer was finally brought to trial.

Now, when people talk about Trinity Lutheran, they say, "Oh, isn't that the church where the young janitor was killed?"

For a long time, Paul felt partially to blame for Brian's death. *We should have made the church more secure, or we should never have allowed Brian to work there alone in the evenings.* In the months following the tragedy, Stan Malsberger did everything he could to make the building more secure. Tempered glass was placed in all the basement windows. The old lock on the parking lot door was finally replaced and new keys were issued. A security alarm system was installed in the building. Paul did everything he could to calm the congregation and comfort the family. He knew there was no answer but he kept wondering why God allowed this to happen.

Paul admitted to himself that he was as much in need of forgiveness and peace as the members of his church. After lunch he opened his Bible and read the gospel verses assigned for the coming Sunday. The story of Jesus calming the sea seemed most appropriate for all he and the congregation had been through.

> On that day, when evening had come, he said to them, "Let us go across to the other side." And leaving the crowd, they took Jesus with them, just as he was, in the boat. And other boats were with him. And a great storm of wind arose, and the waves beat into the boat, so that the boat was already filling. But he was in the stern asleep on the cushion; and they woke him and said to him, "Teacher, do you not care if we perish?" And he awoke and rebuked the wind, and said to the sea, "Peace! Be still!" And the wind ceased, and there was a great calm. He said

to them, "Why were you afraid? Have you no faith?" And they were filled with awe, and said to one another, "Who then is this, that even wind and sea obey him?" Mark 4:35-41

Paul picked up his pen and began scribbling notes and phrases on a lined yellow pad. Once or twice each year the Spirit would put him in a mood for poetry. This morning he was moved to write in a limerick style.

In our gospel today
It's quite fair to say
The disciples became rather queasy.
"Have faith," we could tell them
But that wouldn't quell them
Even if to us it sounds easy.

Jesus woke with surprise,
Spoke to sea and the skies,
"Be still and be calm and at peace."
At once they obeyed;
Down the waves laid,
And the raging wind did cease.

Waves beat on the boat;
It was barely afloat,
With the Lord on the cushion asleep.
"Master, waken, arise!
Rub the sleep from your eyes!
We're about to sink in the deep."

The disciples in awe
Could not believe what they saw.
He said to them, "Why do you fear?
When storms come your way,
Forget not to pray;
Remember, your God is near."

"Lord, don't you care?
You don't easily scare,
But we're afraid we will perish.
While you take your rest
Our faith's put to the test,
For our life is something we cherish."

Each looked at his brother
And said to the other,
"Who is this who speaks to the sea?
The wind and the wave
Seem to behave
When Jesus makes his decree."

Paul had been writing and rewriting for over an hour. *So what is this story saying to us?* Paul asked himself. After a few minutes' reflection, again he put pen to paper.

If God can make the wind and waves,
And rule the sky and sea,
Won't he also calm the fears
That trouble you and me?

Some still hide among the crowds
That wait upon the land.
And some set sail without the Lord,
No Bible in their hand.

Jim Bornzin

Ambassadors of Christ, we're called
To witness to the lost;
To love, forgive, and reconcile,
No matter what the cost.

The price was paid by Jesus
Who died on Calvary's tree,
Who calmed the storm and wind and
waves,
All for you and me.

Remember, though our Lord may sleep,
He knows how much we fear the deep.
With each storm our faith is tested.
On the cushion Jesus rested.
Wake him, if you must, by praying.
"Peace, be still!" we'll hear him saying.

Paul glanced at the clock, two fifty-five in the afternoon. He had been writing since twelve-thirty. He said a quick good-by to Carol, and headed for home to wait for the boys who would be walking home from school.

After Brian Holloway's death, a group of members felt it never would have happened if it weren't for the church's emphasis on neighborhood ministry. Terry Mankovic, the intruder, had come to one of Trinity's community fairs, and cased the church for easy entry during the open house tour. The church members who didn't like community ministry began to blame the pastor for Brian's death. Paul suspected there were other reasons they didn't like him and wanted him to leave, but that was a convenient argument to use against his ministry.

Following an uproar at the congregation's annual meeting Stan and Beth Malsberger, George and Louise Downing, Liz Sterling, Charlie Schoen, and two other couples met to discuss "the pastoral situation." Stan led off the conversation. "I've been doing some research in our constitution and found out it's not easy to get rid of a pastor in the Lutheran church. It requires some pretty serious offense. You can't just say you disagree with him."

Stan waited to let his words sink in. "Is the pastor having an affair that anyone knows about?" he asked. Everyone glanced nervously around the room. "Molesting kids?" he asked in joking exaggeration. "No, I'm half serious. We need something more than difference of opinion about his leadership."

"Has he taken any money from the church?" Beth asked.

"We're not in great shape financially, but the treasurer's report was reviewed by an audit committee; so I don't think we'll get anywhere with that approach," George replied.

The wheels were turning in Liz's head. *Embezzlement, hmm . . . Make the pastor look guilty . . . Rick Rousch's term is about to expire . . . a new treasurer will be needed . . .*

"What about that other article in the constitution, the one about 'ineffective ministry'?" Louise inquired. "It says if the pastor's leadership is deemed to be ineffective, the bishop can replace him."

"Well, that's what I've been saying all along," Charlie Schoen spoke up. "All his darn outreach to the neighborhood has only resulted in one thing, our best janitor getting killed!"

A week later, Stan and George had an appointment with the bishop to express their concerns about Pastor Paul Walker's ineffective leadership. The bishop listened patiently and promised to send a reconciliation team to interview members and explore possibilities.

As it turned out, the bishop was not surprised that a backlash had occurred. He had attended Brian's memorial service, and promised Paul his support, knowing that tragedy often tears families and congregations apart. The Holloway family moved away some time after Christmas. The following Easter, conflict in the congregation was brought to an end when the bishop came for worship and urged the congregation to support their pastor and continue their mission-oriented ministry. Several families, including the Downings and Malsbergers, left the church to worship elsewhere.

Liz Sterling, however, was not the kind to give up. She was elected treasurer of the congregation, replacing Rick Rousch, who had served faithfully for two full terms, a total of six years.

Paul was grateful for the bishop's support and encouragement. As a pastor, he was sad to lose several families from the church, and at the same time, somewhat relieved. One of his seminary professors insisted his students memorize and repeat this maxim every day of their ministry: *You can't please everybody!* Paul had been repeating it five times a day for the past six months!

It was also during these months that Paul heard for the first time a Christian song by Laura Story, called "Blessings." He made a copy of the lyrics and hung them on a wall in his office.

It was several months before the intruder who killed Brian Holloway was caught, and nearly a year after Brian's death before he was brought to trial. Terry Mankovic was found guilty of voluntary manslaughter and sentenced to fifteen to twenty years in prison. A painful chapter in Trinity's history was officially brought to a close, but the wounds would take years to heal, and the scars would be a permanent part of Paul's ministry.

5

My name is **Michael Greenwood**. I'm a senior at Weston High. I've been writing this journal for almost a year now. You may have heard of Brian Holloway, who worked part-time as the janitor at Trinity? He was my best friend ever. He's the main reason I started this journal. If you're an older person, it might help you understand how hard it is for kids growing up these days. Sure has been hard for me the past year or two!

I'm a pretty cool guy actually. At least I thought I was when I first saw Kathy Stiletto . . . honest to God, that's her real name! I'm not making it up. And she lived up to it . . . put a dagger through my heart.

It was our sophomore year. Kathy transferred from Nashville, Tennessee. We all thought . . . that's pretty cool! I've never been to Nashville, but I love country music. My best friend, Brian Holloway, and I started talking about how pretty she was . . . in a scary sort of way, you know, like . . . you'd like to get to know her, but you're scared to talk to her? She hung with several girls, not the most popular girls in the class. Maybe they wanted to hang with her, like Stiletto *wannabees*. There was a lot of talk *about* her, but except for her girlfriends, almost nobody talked *to* her.

She was mysterious, sort of friendly, but hard to get to know. I made a bet with Brian that I could get a date with her before he did. Like I said, I thought I was pretty cool, so I went up to her after class one day and said, "Hey, Kathy, I'm Michael, welcome to Weston."

She smiled and said, "Hey, Michael, you're cute!" Then she reached out, put her hand on my head, and tousled my hair. That really took guts! It made me feel like a dork, but I kinda liked that she touched me.

I asked if she liked Weston and she said it was okay. Then I asked her about Nashville, and she laughed. "Everybody thinks Nashville is this way cool place to live. It's not any different from here really. You know, like you've GOT to go to school! And Nashville parents are jerks, just like here!" That made me laugh.

Oh, yeah, parents . . . I should tell you about my parents, but I can't. I don't even remember who they were hardly. I was five when I was taken away from my mom and placed in a foster home. All I remember about my mom was sometimes she was real sweet and sometimes she was real mean, and she slept a lot . . . even during the day. My dad was a long haul truck driver so I don't remember him much at all.

My second family was real nice . . . I thought I was adopted 'cause I lived with them for nine years, 'til I was fourteen, even called them Mom and Dad. Really bummed me out when they told the state worker they couldn't do it anymore. I thought they meant they had had enough foster kids and didn't want to take in any more. They were constantly telling me they were getting too old to have any more kids. They had fourteen in all. Not all at once, mind you. There were pictures of them on the mantel. Mom and Dad looked really young in the pictures. So, anyway, I thought they meant they couldn't take in any more foster kids, but then the case worker took me aside for a long talk. She explained that Mom was having some health issues. Dad was concerned about medical expenses. They had asked the state to find a new place for me. Like I said, I was really bummed. So the state placed me in a new home.

I'm with my new foster parents now, but I don't call them Mom and Dad, I just call them Jack and Charlotte. They've got four other foster kids. I'm the oldest. Next, there's two girls, eleven and twelve, but they're from two different families. The youngest are the twins, two boys, four years old. I get a kick out of them. They're really wild little guys. Jack and Charlotte have their hands full raising them! The girls are just . . . I don't know . . . just girls. You know, they whisper and giggle constantly, just like sisters.

I haven't got the slightest what they're laughin' about all the time. I guess they're best friends; that's a good thing. I know it's hard not being with your real parents. So, I'm pretty much on my own. Charlotte enjoys the girls and gives them lots of attention. And she's doing the best she can with the twins; sometimes they're a pain!

I spend a lot of time in my room upstairs. It gets really hot up there in the summer; seems like the air-conditioning cools downstairs but never gets up to my room. So I go over to Brian's a lot. He's got really cool parents. Now that's what I call a NORMAL family! At least it's what I always thought a real family should be. The Holloways are really nice to me. Sometimes they let me stay and have dinner with them. Then Brian and I do homework together. It's okay with Jack and Charlotte as long as I call and let them know where I am. I think Charlotte and Marge talk sometimes on the phone when Brian and I aren't around.

Now what was I writing about? Oh, yeah, Kathy Stiletto. Oh, yeah, I won the bet. For a while Kathy teased me constantly, especially in the school cafeteria. She'd come by my table and tousle my hair. "Hey, Michael!" Then she'd laugh and walk away with her friends. She was driving me crazy. One day, after school, she ran up behind me and Brian, and hit me on the back of the head. I didn't see her coming. Scared the shit out of me. She laughed and said, "Hey, Michael, wanna go to a movie Saturday?" I said, "Sure, I'll call you." So that's how I won the bet with Brian and got the first date with Stiletto.

Kathy really seemed to like me. And I thought I was the luckiest guy in the world. That was my junior year. By then, Brian had a girlfriend too. The four of us met at football games and yelled our heads off! We went to basketball games together. I asked Kathy to the Winter Dance and she looked so hot! We danced and danced. I couldn't keep my hands off her! When she went to the girls' room, I waited in the hall. We ducked into a corner and started making out. When the dance was over I started to drive her home, but first I drove out by the lake. I hope Jack and Charlotte never read this journal, 'cause that night was the first time Kathy and I did it. It was unreal!

I'll never forget spring of my junior year. I'm telling Brian how in love I am with Kathy, and he keeps telling me to slow down. He doesn't get it. He

31

and his girlfriend are "saving themselves," he says. Kathy and I spent a lot of time together that spring. We did it in Jack's car; we did it in the park one night on a blanket. Turns out, Brian was right. I was an idiot. I was thinking Kathy and I might get married after we graduated. How could I have been so naïve?

Then, this last summer, Kathy and her parents went back to Nashville for a visit with family down there. When she came back, it seemed like everything changed. We both had summer jobs. I was working at Napa Auto Parts, stocking shelves and grabbing parts for customer orders. She was doing something in the clothing section at Wal-Mart. When we did get together some evenings, she wasn't hot for me like she was before.

Senior year I was looking forward to being with Kathy at games and dances. It was going to be a great year! I should have seen it coming. A few weeks after school started, Brian told me he'd seen Kathy hanging out with Kevin, the quarterback from our football team. I couldn't believe it! Kevin's a jerk! He's so in love with himself! The first game of the season was against the East Chicago Mustangs. At school on Friday I casually said to Kathy, "See you at the game tonight?"

She said, "Yeah, you probably will . . . but I'll be sitting with my friends." She turned to walk away.

The way she said it . . . really ticked me off. As she walked away I hollered, "I thought we'd sit together like we did last year!"

Glancing over her shoulder she replied, "Sorry, Michael, maybe next game." Somehow, she didn't sound like she meant it.

Sure enough, that night, Kathy and a bunch of girls were there in the stadium. She didn't see me; she never even looked for me. But I saw her and her Kathy *wannabees*, screaming and yelling every time KEVIN made a run or completed a pass! It made me sick! Something was going on between her and that creep. I didn't call her that night, or all weekend. And she never called me. When I saw her in school on Monday I asked her, "What's with you and Kevin?"

She looked me in the eyes with kind of a sad, pathetic look. Then she reached up and tousled my hair like she always did. Then she smiled and said, "Michael, I hate to tell you this, but you and I are through. I'm going with Kevin now." Just like that. Stuck the dagger in my heart. Kathy Stiletto. Can you believe that name?

I couldn't wait to talk to Brian. I was dying inside. He had tried to warn me. I called him that night after supper and asked if I could hang out at his house for a while. He said, "Sure. C'mon over."

Brian was like a brother; and his parents made me feel like part of his family, a normal family, something I'd always dreamed of. For weeks, all I could talk about was Kathy Stiletto. And Brian just kept saying, "You'll get over her." I don't think he understood the bond Kathy and I had. It was really deep. At least it was for me. I'd never felt that way about anybody. I was physically sick. It's hard to explain. My stomach hurt. I couldn't sleep at night. I kept thinking about Kathy and what might have been. I guess Brian told his mom about me and Kathy. She felt really bad for me. She made cookies for me and sent them home with me.

A few years ago when Brian turned sixteen, his family took me to the County Fair. Brian and I rode on rides for hours! His little sister Sarah went on a lot of them with us. She was fun because she was so scared. She'd scream bloody murder! Finally, we went home. Mrs. Holloway made a big dinner with Brian's favorite barbeque ribs. Then she brought out a birthday cake with sixteen candles. She told Brian to make a wish, and just as he was about to blow, his dad made a joke. Brian laughed and only four candles went out. He blew again, but he was still laughing, and only three more candles went out. "Bet THAT wish won't come true!" his dad said. When Brian caught his breath, he blew out the rest of the candles. What none of them knew was that I had made a wish too. I wished I had a normal family like Brian's.

Anyway, that fall I went to football games with Brian and Theresa again instead of Kathy. From where we sat we could always see Stiletto and her buddies jumping and cheering for good ol' Kevin. I sort of swore off girls. Brian and his girlfriend were still "saving themselves for marriage." Brian had big plans for college and got accepted at Purdue. I was so bummed about being dumped by Kathy I couldn't study. I flunked two classes . . . shit! Didn't graduate . . . shit! I told Charlotte and Jack I was sorry. I just didn't care anymore. Charlotte called the school office and they made me talk to the counselor. He listened pretty good. Jack and Charlotte said I had to graduate. They insisted that I'd be attending school one more quarter in the fall to make up the credits I needed to graduate. So, in June of my senior year, I attended Brian's graduation ceremony with Bob and Marge Holloway. His sister Sarah was there too. We were all very proud of Brian.

This summer I worked again at Napa, like I had the summer before, but I had my driver's license now, so in addition to stocking shelves, they let me do deliveries in town. Brian had a part-time job too. He was the janitor at the Lutheran church. He'd go over there on Monday after school and clean up the place. Sometimes he'd go during the week. And always on Friday or Saturday night, so it would look nice on Sunday morning. He also worked part-time at a veterinary clinic taking care of dogs and cats mostly. He said he really loved animals and wanted to go to college and study to be a real veterinarian.

So now you'll see why I'm writing this. The counselor at school said I should put it all down in a journal, and at first, I wouldn't do it. But after what happened to Brian, I bought a spiral notebook like I used at school and I started writing and writing.

On a hot Friday night in August Brian went to clean the church like he always did. Some idiot had broken a window and climbed into the church kitchen. I guess he wanted to rob the place. Can you imagine? Robbing a church? How low is that? So when Brian got there, he found the broken glass and, according to the police, he swept it up. Then he must have heard something, dropped the broom and dust pan, and chased the guy through the fellowship hall and up the stairs to the exit. They fought on the stairs and the scumbag stabbed Brian. The police said they found Brian at the bottom of the steps and he bled to death . . . . Jesus!

The word spread fast and I heard about it on Saturday. I couldn't believe it. I went in my room and couldn't stop crying. I'd hold it for a while, then I couldn't help it, the tears just kept coming. Charlotte and Jack were pretty good about it. They knew Brian was my best friend. All they said was, "We'll leave you alone, but you come talk about it when you feel ready." Monday, Charlotte kept banging on my door and said I had to get up and go to work. I didn't feel like it, but maybe it was good I did. It got my mind off Brian a little bit, and I didn't want the guys at Napa to see me cry.

A week later they had Brian's memorial service at Trinity Lutheran Church where it all happened. Practically our whole class was there! I didn't realize Brian was that popular. I felt really bad for the Holloways. His mom said I could sit with them since Brian and I had been best friends. Theresa sat with her parents. Mrs. Holloway cried almost the whole time. His dad looked dead. His sister Sarah was really brave. She's only fourteen. She got up to the microphone and talked about Brian and his love of animals, and she said how much she loved him. That's when everyone cried. I got up too, and told how Brian and I had played a joke on our coach. I loved Brian's sense of humor!

After Labor Day I was really in a shit hole. All I could think about was Brian. He and I had talked about this being our last summer together. He meant because he was going to Purdue. I never thought it would really be our "last summer together, forever." That's when I started writing . . . about Brian . . . about Kathy . . . about everything that was happening.

So, here's what happened next. I went back to school in the fall. I had an appointment every week with the school counselor. I went to work. There's a guy who repairs cars out of his garage at home. A lot of people know about him and take their cars there, like for oil change which he does real cheap, or minor repairs. I take parts there all the time. He lives just a block from Brian's house. The first week of school I had to deliver some parts to this guy's garage. I drove past Brian's house and I started to cry. After I delivered the parts, I drove back to Brian's and parked in front. I sat there for the longest time, just staring at his house and remembering Brian. Finally I got out of the car and went up to the front door, and Mrs. Holloway answered. I think she could tell I had been crying. I didn't know what to say. She told me to come in. We went in the kitchen and she poured me some milk and gave me some of my favorite cookies. I started to cry again. Mrs. Holloway said, "That's okay, Michael. I miss Brian too." We talked for a while; then she wrapped up the cookies like she always did, and sent them home with me.

That night I got out my journal again. There were pages and pages about Kathy, and then pages about Michael. I wrote it all down like the counselor said I should, you know, "try to get all your feelings out." That night I wrote for a couple of hours. I couldn't fall asleep because I couldn't stop thinking. At midnight, Jack hollered, "Turn off the light!" *I wish I had a real family. I wish I had Brian back.*

6

The state prison was not Paul's favorite place to visit. He had just come out through the gate of the prison into the visitors' parking lot. He was emotionally drained by his visit with Terry Mankovic. Terry had been found guilty of voluntary manslaughter in the death of Brian Holloway. Cheri had begged him not to visit Terry again. Paul had visited Terry shortly after his arrest because he wanted to get some idea of the kind of person Terry was. He was also curious to see if Terry was feeling any remorse over Brian's death. If so, Paul felt obligated to bring a word of forgiveness from God, even if Paul himself wasn't ready to forgive.

Now it was official. Terry had been convicted of manslaughter and would spend at least fifteen years in prison. In spite of Cheri's cautious counsel, something in Paul was telling him to visit Terry one more time. The words of Jesus were haunting him, "I was naked and you clothed me, I was sick and you visited me, I was in prison and you came to me." Paul hated the prison environment, fences, gates, guards . . . waiting to see a prisoner. Nevertheless, Paul believed he should "walk the talk."

During the visit Paul asked about Terry's family and learned that his father had died when Terry was only fourteen years old. "Your dad must have been quite young. What caused his death?" Paul asked.

"My dad was walking to work one night and was hit by a delivery truck turning into an alley."

"That must have been an awful blow to your family," Paul responded sympathetically.

37

"Yeah, my mom took it really hard. She had to start working. I was only in eighth grade and I had a little brother in fourth grade. I was mad about losing my dad. Really mad! Mad at the whole world!"

Paul nodded. It didn't excuse what Terry had done to Brian, but it helped Paul understand why Terry was prone to trouble. Before leaving the prison, Paul offered to pray with Terry who said that would be okay. Paul said a short prayer and concluded with the Lord's Prayer. He was only slightly surprised when Terry joined in, praying along with him. As they finished with *forever and ever, Amen,* Terry looked at Paul and said, "You know, Pastor, sometimes when I say that prayer I feel like I'm praying to my dad instead of God."

"Why's that?" Paul asked.

"You know, *Our Father who art in heaven.* My father died and is in heaven, so I kinda feel like I'm talking to him."

"Of course, of course," Paul stammered. Paul's dad was still living and such a thought had never crossed his mind.

When the visit ended Paul made his way back through security doors, through the waiting area, and out to the parking lot. He couldn't stop thinking about the words "Our Father." What would those words mean to a young girl whose father had sexually abused her? What would they mean to a child whose dad had run off with another woman? What would they mean to a child whose mother died in childbirth and whose father gave the infant up for adoption?

Paul had always thought of Jesus speaking to his heavenly Father: a compassionate Father, a trustworthy Father, a wise Father, a loving Father, a tender and intimate Father. Surely that is how Jesus wanted us to think of God. Paul believed Jesus was trying to reshape the traditional Jewish image of a jealous deity who demanded obedience to his authority and power. Paul also believed that Jesus wanted to include Gentiles in the family of God. People of every race, gender, social class . . . even those of every religion or philosophical persuasion . . . should be considered part of God's family, whether they know it or not, whether they believe it or not.

Having been raised in a loving family, Paul liked that image for God's people. We are all brothers and sisters, children of God. Our faith is supposed to mature along with everything else. When we are "little children" we should be taught about God who provides love and guidance, rules and boundaries, just like a loving parent. The commandments are given lovingly, for our protection; not arbitrarily, because God demands obedience. As we grow, God gives us more and more freedom, expecting us to use our intelligence, common sense, and eventually wisdom.

Sitting in his car, staring at the tall fence topped by razor wire, Paul realized how much freedom God gives us. We aren't puppets on a string. We are free to do all kinds of horrible things. God must be terribly sad when his children fail. But it must make God extremely joyful and proud when we choose to do kind and loving things. Paul prayed for Terry, for Bob and Marge and Sarah Holloway, for Terry's mom, though he had never met her. He prayed for the detectives who had arrested Terry, Sean Asplund and his partner Chad. He prayed for Maria Olivera who had given the police their first lead and who was now a member of Trinity.

Paul turned the key in the ignition and started his car. Before putting it in gear he prayed for his wife Cheri and sons Chip and Randy. He prayed for his congregation, Trinity Lutheran Church.

> *Heavenly Father, may we become the family of God you desire us to be. Help us, by your Holy Spirit, to love you above anything else. And help us to love one another, even when we are not easy to love. Help me to be a faithful shepherd, a faithful father and husband. Forgive me for all my failings. Help me to proclaim your good news boldly, and then help me walk the walk. Amen.*

PART 2

7

Liz Sterling strolled into the church office a few minutes after noon. It was her lunch hour, and she could usually get a few items taken care of at church before eating and returning to Weston Realty. She had been serving as treasurer of Trinity for a couple of years. Liz didn't mind the routine, preparing a monthly report for the congregation council, coming to the church office once a week or so to cut checks and pay the bills.

Several checks needed to be signed, and last Sunday's offering needed to be recorded on the church balance sheet. Over the lunch hour was also a time when Pastor Paul left the office, and she could do a little snooping, if Carol the secretary, wasn't watching. Liz discovered that Paul had a habit of writing notes to himself on small slips of paper. It helped remind him of things he needed to do, and the notes were more visible lying on the desk in the open than waiting for the computer to boot up, or searching through his desk calendar. Liz pulled the checkbook from the file cabinet, sat down at the table in Carol's office, and began signing checks.

Carol stood up, "Liz, would you mind grabbing the phone if it rings? I need to step out a minute."

"Sure, Carol; no problem."

As the secretary headed for the restroom Liz glanced into Paul's office and noticed several notes on his desk. She walked over, scooped up the notes, and tucked them in her purse. *When Paul returned that afternoon or the next day he would probably think they had fallen on the floor, or been dropped in the waste basket, or that he had placed them somewhere else. He is so absent-minded he probably writes notes to remind himself to go to the john! Ha! Speaking of the john, I'd better get out of here before Carol comes back.* Liz finished signing the checks, and was putting the checkbook back in the drawer when Carol returned. She said goodbye to Carol and hurried out the office door.

Back at the realty office Liz glanced at the notes she had taken from Paul's desk. One was a reminder to call Darrel Thomas, re: Immigration Committee; another, the name Jana Nygaard and a date for her surgery; and the third, a short grocery list which appeared to be in Cheri's handwriting. *Oh, this is going to frustrate the heck out of him,* Liz thought as she gleefully tossed them into her wastebasket.

Liz had been working very hard since taking over as treasurer. First, she was delighted to find an old discretionary fund which had been set up for Pastor Bjornstad years ago. It had apparently fallen into disuse and been forgotten. An old book of checks was tucked into a file folder which had been passed on to her from Rick Rousch. Working from home one evening, she set it up for internet banking but kept it separate from the other funds for Trinity Lutheran. For a password, she used Paul's middle name and the numbers of his birthday. She said nothing to Paul about her discovery. Nor did she list the fund on her monthly report. Next, she began a monthly transfer from the General Fund into the Pastor's Discretionary Fund. She varied the amount transferred and listed it as a bill paid to PDF on the treasurer's report. Only once during the past year did someone from the council ask what PDF meant. She lied, saying it was for office supplies; and no further questions were asked.

Now, all she needed to decide was how and when to remove the money from the fund. It gave her great joy to know that there was a copy of Paul Walker's signature in her file at Weston Realty. She still had it from the signing of the *Agreement to Purchase* form for the Walker's new home. After a few months, Liz decided to write a check from the Pastor's Discretionary Fund and forge Paul's signature. She made the check out to CASH for $500, carefully copied Paul's handwriting, and took it to the bank. With an air of confidence she asked to speak to the branch manager. Her professional nametag from Weston Realty read LIZ.

She shook hands with the manager. "Hi! I'm Liz Sterling from Weston Realty. I'm also the treasurer for our church, Trinity Lutheran, which has several accounts here. Our pastor is trying to help one of our church families," she lowered her voice to a whisper, "but he wants to make sure they remain anonymous. He asked if I would come here to cash this check from his discretionary fund. Can you help me?"

The manager examined the check. Everything appeared in order. "Certainly, Ms. Sterling. Step over here to one of the tellers."

That was easy, Liz thought to herself. *Guess I'll just let this little fund build up a while and see how much I can save for a rainy day!* Liz thanked the teller and tucked five crisp $100 bills into her purse.

That afternoon, Paul returned to the office to see if Carol had any more messages or questions for him. He also wanted to pick up the note which Cheri had given him this morning. He was not about to forget those groceries *this time*! He glanced across his desk. *Where is that list? I know I put it here this morning.*

"Carol, have you seen my grocery list anywhere? Maybe I laid it on the table in your office?"

"No, Pastor, I haven't seen it."

Paul checked his pockets. "Darn it! I'm getting more and more forgetful. I'm way too young for senility!" Carol chuckled in response to Paul's self-deprecating humor.

Paul returned to his desk, reluctantly dialed Cheri's number at the law firm where she worked, and confessed he had lost the note. "Can you please tell me what I needed to pick up at the grocery store before going home? And don't worry; I'll be there in time to meet Randy and Chip after school."

8

Reiner and Tillie Holtz joined Trinity

with a small group of new members in September that year. The first thing people noticed about Reiner was his thick German accent. The second was his nervous eyes, which glanced back and forth constantly. And the third thing members noticed was the smell of tobacco on his breath. What people noticed about Tillie was that she never spoke when Reiner was around. She almost appeared to be afraid of her husband. The dresses she wore dated back to the 1940s and 50s, many of them inherited from her mother. The children at church sometimes pointed and giggled at her lace-up "grandma shoes." Pastor Paul had noted all these characteristics and was curious to learn more about their background. He hoped that a welcoming church community might help both of them to be more at ease.

About a week before the reception of new members, Paul called them on the phone to ask if he could make a visit at their home. Reiner answered gruffly and seemed reluctant to allow the pastor anything more than a casual acquaintance. Paul mentioned his visits with other new members and told Reiner how much he would appreciate the opportunity to get better acquainted. Finally, Reiner agreed to a visit. A date was set for Thursday evening before the Sunday reception at church.

Thursday morning was a beautiful September day. The cool air was crisp and breezy. The weather forecast seemed odd for this time of year. A warm front was moving up from the gulf bringing warmer temperatures and the chance of rain. Paul could hardly believe how the air turned warmer as the sun was going down that afternoon. After dinner, he drove to the Holtz's

Jim Bornzin

home and parked on the street. A full moon shone above the house, lighting the edges of billowing clouds, and casting ominous shadows across the lawn. The home seemed torn from the pages of a Transylvania tourist brochure, with twin brick towers on each corner. A warm, yet eerie, glow radiated through the leaded glass of the front windows.

Paul climbed three steps and rang the bell. Reiner welcomed him into the living room. He hung Paul's jacket on an old-fashioned coat hook near the front door. Tillie rose from her high-backed chair and shook his hand. Her broad smile put the pastor at ease. Paul was amazed at the warmth and charm of the turn-of-the-century décor, turn of the last century. The windows were draped with lace curtains. Crocheted doilies covered the end tables and the arms of sofa and chairs. A tiffany lamp stood in one corner. The house was quiet until the sound of thunder rolled in the distance, sending a strange chill up Paul's spine.

As soon as they were seated in the living room, Reiner lit his pipe and blew the smoke slowly into the air. Paul learned that both Tillie and Reiner had been born in Germany, Reiner in 1940 and Tillie in 1946, making them 52 and 46 respectively. Paul had been certain from appearances that they were both in their sixties. Reiner began talking about "ze War," the Nazis, and his strict father, who had been a colonel under General Heimlich Himmler. Reiner was a walking encyclopedia of Nazi Germany.

"Wasn't Himmler in charge of the Gestapo?" Paul asked.

"Yes, and my father was a very loyal Nazi at first. He was promoted several times within the party, eventually becoming an assistant to General Himmler. You zee, my father was responsible for ze records of Himmler's orders. My father was a stickler for details, what we would now call 'compulsive.' In Germany, zat trait was admired. After we came to America, and I was older, my father told me about his role in ze Reich, und how he grew more and more upset about ze killing of thousands of innocent people. At first he went along with prison camps for ze Jews, but then they started killing ze mentally ill and Catholics, and Poles, and anyone whom Hitler believed needed to be eliminated in order to 'purify' ze world. My father began having second thoughts. He began keeping a duplicate set of documents which he hid in our home."

"That must have been very risky," Paul commented.

"I'm sure it was." Reiner struck another match and held it to his pipe. "When ze war ended, Himmler ordered ze records to be burned, and my father obeyed. As you may know, Himmler committed suicide; und after his death, my father handed over his secret set of documents to ze Allies. I sink he was very ashamed of his part in ze atrocities. My father assured me he did not order ze executions, nor did he participate in zem. 'But I did nothing to stop zem either,' he confessed to mother and me when I was in my teens."

During the entire hour Paul was there, Tillie smiled, but never spoke. At one point she rose and went to the kitchen. In a few moments she returned with an old aluminum coffee pot on a tray with three cups, a bowl of sugar, and small pitcher of cream. She placed them on the coffee table in front of Paul and smiled. "Please help yourself," she said as she nervously wiped her hands on her apron. "There's cream there if you like," she said and took her seat.

"Thank you, Tillie," Paul replied. He reached over and poured himself about half a cup of stout black coffee. Reiner poured himself a full cup and placed it on his end table. Then Tillie stood up again and poured herself a cup, stirring in cream and sugar.

Paul shared a brief history of Trinity and told them a little about his family, and how he and Cheri had decided to come to Weston seven years ago. Reiner and Tillie listened appreciatively. When Reiner placed his pipe in the ashtray, Paul glanced at his watch. "It's getting late and I should probably be going. I'd like to offer a prayer for you, if you don't mind." After the prayer, they stood and Paul moved toward the door. "Thank you both for your hospitality," Paul said as he slipped on his jacket. "I appreciate your telling me so much about your father, Reiner; and Tillie, thank you for the coffee."

"Ach, think nothing of it," Reiner replied. Tillie stood behind Reiner in the doorway and gave a small wave as Paul stepped off the porch and headed for his car. At the curb, he glanced back. Reiner and Tillie were still standing in the open doorway. The air was warm and humid. The clouds were still racing across the moon which had risen even higher. But so far, no trace of rain. Paul took one more look around the neighborhood. *No werewolves in sight . . .* Paul thought as he slipped behind the wheel . . . *but the history of Nazi Germany is certainly alive and well in this place.*

*   *   *

For the first few months, everyone made an effort to get to know Reiner and Tillie. Reiner politely refused invitations to usher, read the lessons, or attend the adult Sunday Forum. Tillie's curly white hair, deeply-lined face, and pleasant smile made her quite approachable, but Tillie politely declined to join a women's circle. During the coffee time Tillie often found her way into the kitchen to help the women who were serving coffee and cookies. She would place cream and sugar on the serving table, or bring a stack of paper napkins. She quietly picked up a dish towel and began drying dishes coming hot out of the dishwasher. She held the dishes carefully in the towel and stacked them on the shelf.

On a chilly evening in Lent, Paul made his second visit at the Holtz's home. Tillie served him a very stout cup of coffee. Reiner asked if he'd like a little schnapps, but Paul declined. "During my last visit, you told me a lot about your parents and you talked about World War II. I'd like to hear, what brought your family to the United States?" Paul inquired.

Reiner tipped his head down and peered over his spectacles. Then he reached over to the end table and picked up his pipe. "After ze war, my family came to America, hoping to start a new life." Reiner packed tobacco carefully into the pipe and lit it, inhaling and exhaling slowly. Paul felt he was stalling for time as he tried to decide how much to share. "To tell ze truth, I think my father felt fortunate that he wasn't involved in ze war crimes trials. It was probably because of his cooperation in handing over ze secret documents. I was only ten years old when we left Germany and landed in a German neighborhood in Chicago. Tillie was in high school when I met her, and we were wed in 1963."

"Do you have any children?" Paul asked.

Reiner looked at Tillie and didn't speak. Apparently, he wanted her to answer this question. Tillie fidgeted with her hands and looked from

Reiner to Paul. "I learned from my doctor that I couldn't have any children," she said nervously. Her head dropped and she appeared embarrassed, perhaps even ashamed.

"I'm sorry to hear that," Paul said softly. "And what brought you to Weston?" Paul asked, still looking at Tillie, and hoping she would answer.

"Vell, Pastor, I tell you how it vas," Reiner continued. "After getting my Masters degree in history at Valparaiso University, I began work on my PhD at Notre Dame. I taught zer for a while, but I just didn't see eye to eye with those Catholics. To make a long story short, I applied for a teaching position at Weston High in ze history department, and I've been here ever since."

"And if you don't mind my asking, what brought you to Trinity Lutheran?"

"Ya. Ya. You probably think I belong in the Missouri Synod because of my German accent. Ya, zat's where we were married in Chicago, and we joined the Missouri church here in Weston. The truth is . . . we just didn't get along there." Reiner glanced nervously at Tillie, and again, her eyes dropped downward.

"Pastor Walker, did you ever hear of the Jewish conspiracy?" Reiner asked, changing the subject.

"Not sure, Reiner. What conspiracy are you talking about?"

"I know zis isn't a popular opinion these days, but my father was convinced zat before ze Holocaust, Jews were trying to take control of ze world."

"That's a pretty wild idea, Reiner. What made him believe that?"

"Oh, it's not wild at all, Pastor. It was very clear, not only to Hitler and my father, but to many people all over ze world. Jews have been resettling in countries for many centuries. Everywhere zey go, zey own businesses and banks. Zey are professional people who know how to manage money and control the economy of the community. Zey were becoming very powerful in Germany, and in Poland and Russia, in most of Europe, even in America!"

"Oh Reiner, that may have been a theory in the early twentieth century, but it certainly isn't credible any longer."

"Wait a minute, Pastor, have you ever been to New York? Jews run ze biggest city in our nation. Have you been to California? Hollywood is run by Jews."

"I'm sorry, Reiner, I don't want to get into a debate, but from my understanding of history, the Jews have always been a persecuted people. That's why they have emigrated all over the world. Some Jewish people are very wealthy; I don't deny that. But I can't believe there is a conspiracy to rule the world."

"Well, I'll tell you one zing. Nobody trusts zem! Zat is why zey won't be able to take over!"

"Not to argue, Reiner, but I trust them. Rabbi Isaac Chevitz, here in Weston, is one of my best friends." Paul was becoming very uncomfortable with the direction of the conversation. After a few more minutes of small talk, he excused himself, and drove home, his mind reviewing the conversation and everything else he had seen. When Cheri greeted him with a hug, he did his best to shift his focus from Reiner Holtz to his own home and family. For the rest of the evening Paul thought about Reiner and Tillie. The visit continued to haunt him for many months.

9

The highlight of October was

homecoming. For Randy it was the football game, but for Chip it was the homecoming parade. The trumpet Chip was using during his freshman year was an inexpensive, second-hand instrument Paul and Cheri had bought when he was taking lessons in junior high. Chip had begged for a new trumpet last summer when he tried out for the high school marching band, but Cheri wasn't sure they should spend several hundred dollars unless Chip was fully committed. Of course, being in the marching band was an honor, and Chip's excitement was understandable, but would he stick with it? Finally Paul made a promise. "If you continue playing throughout the year, we will buy you a new trumpet for marching band next fall."

Chip would not let his dad forget the promise. The following summer he begged, "Please, can I get my new trumpet now?" Every time they drove past the music store, Chip begged, "Can't we just go in and look?" Every time his dad listened to a piece of jazz or classical music, Chip would comment, "Isn't that a great sounding trumpet? I wish I had one like that!"

During one of their summer evening conversations, Paul and Cheri agreed it was time to do the research and go shopping for Chip's new trumpet. They were shocked to see that a really good, concert trumpet could sell for $3000 or more. A used or lower quality trumpet was available for $199, but was not much better than Chip's old one. They looked online and at the local music store and finally decided on a new instrument for $485. The case was another $75.

Chip's birthday was in August, and they knew he desperately wanted it before school began. Paul and Cheri agreed his birthday would be an ideal time to give it to him. The afternoon of his birthday, Chip and Randy were playing softball at a nearby city park. Paul reached underneath Chip's bed, removed the old trumpet, and slid the new case and trumpet in its place. After supper that evening, Cheri reminded Chip that he had to practice trumpet for at least half an hour.

"When you're through practicing," his mom said, "we'll have your birthday cake and you can open your presents."

He went grumbling down the hall to his bedroom. A minute later, his parents were not surprised to hear him shouting, "Oh my God! Oh my God!" Chip came running back down the hall with his new trumpet. "Oh my God, look! Look at my new trumpet!"

"Chip, what did we say about using that expression?" his dad reminded him.

"Sorry, Dad, I was just so excited!"

"Really, Paul, you don't have to be a pastor every minute!" Cheri chided him.

"Thank you, Mom! Thanks, Dad! I love my new trumpet!" He gave them each a hug. "Randy, come here! Look what Mom and Dad got me!"

That evening, Chip practiced for nearly an hour and a half. When he finally came out of his room, he said to his dad, "My mouth hurts."

"Does it hurt too much to eat some birthday cake?" his mom asked jokingly. Chip shot her a don't-be-ridiculous glance as he cut the first big piece for himself.

In September Chip carefully carried his trumpet to school, eager to show his friends and band teacher. After receiving numerous compliments and congratulations, he locked it securely in his locker. Marching Band practice began the second week immediately after school. Drills included all the maneuvers they would perform during halftime at the games. Chip was on top of the world!

Now, in October, Chip could hardly wait for Homecoming Weekend and the big Homecoming Parade in downtown Weston. He had practiced for hours as he had promised his parents he would. That Saturday morning he awoke at 6:30 am and couldn't go back to sleep. He pulled out his music, wrapped his hands around the trumpet and began quietly fingering through the pieces they would play during the parade. At 7:15 he turned to his favorite piece, "When the saints go marchin' in." Without thinking he blew the first few notes, "Oh when the saints . . ." repeat, "go marchin' in . . ." repeat, "Oh when the saints go marchin' in." Suddenly he stopped mid-breath, looked around, and realized he was not fingering silently . . . he was actually blasting his favorite song. Holding the trumpet in one hand, he walked to the door and slowly pulled it open with his other hand. He looked sheepishly down the hallway and there stood his dad in pajamas at the door of their bedroom, simply staring at him.

"I'm so sorry," Chip said, his head dropping and his eyes on the floor.

"What the heck is going on?" yelled Randy as he came out of his bedroom. "You nearly knocked me out of bed!"

"I'm sorry," Chip mumbled again. "I guess I just got carried away."

"Well, we're all up now, that's for sure," Paul sighed. "Guess I'll get dressed." They all went back into their respective bedrooms to get ready for the big parade.

The plan was that Cheri would drive Chip to the high school parking lot at 9:15 where the band was assembling for warm-up. Then Cheri would return home, maybe have a second cup of coffee, and join Paul and Randy for the parade about an hour later. The band would leave the parking lot and move up the street to join the parade starting at 10 am. That was the plan.

What actually happened, however, was something quite different. At nine o'clock, Cheri hollered at Chip, "It's time to go. Let's get moving!" She went to the garage, put the garage door up, and started the car. A moment later, Chip came flying out the door, "I'm coming Mom. I had to make sure my uniform was on right. Our director is really fussy." He jumped into the front seat next to his mom. Cheri checked the rear view mirror to make certain the garage door was up. They backed out of the garage and twenty minutes later pulled up to the school. Chip opened the car door and jumped out. He turned back, eyes searching the front and back car seats. "My trumpet!" he yelled.

"What's wrong with your trumpet?" Cheri asked, trying to keep her tone calm.

"I left it at home!" Chip's voice was filled with panic.

"Get in," his mom said, rolling her eyes and shaking her head. "We'll just have to go back to the house and get it."

Chip jumped back into the car, slammed the door shut, turned to his mom and pleaded, "Please hurry, Mom, our band teacher, Mr. Hanson gets really, really upset when we're late."

Cheri pulled away from the curb and headed home. Traffic around the school was backed up and some of the streets were blocked off because of the parade. They got back home at 9:45, nearly half an hour later. Chip ran into his bedroom while Cheri explained what had happened to Paul and Randy. "Meet me on First Street at our usual corner," Cheri said to Paul as she and Chip got back in the car. "I'll get there as soon as I can."

In a flash they were on their way back to the high school, Chip nearly in tears. "Hurry, Mom, hurry, please!"

"Honey, I'm driving as fast as the law allows." Cheri pulled up to the high school parking lot a few minutes after ten, just as the band was turning the corner and starting down First Street.

"There they go, Mom! Follow 'em! Hurry!"

Cheri started driving toward the corner and was stopped by a police officer holding his arm in the air. "Sorry, m'am, no cars allowed beyond this corner. You'll have to turn left."

"I think I can catch them, Mom." Chip jumped out of the car and started to run after the band.

"Chip!" Cheri hollered. "Your trumpet!"

Chip skidded to a stop, came running back, and grabbed his trumpet out of the case on the back seat. Trumpet in hand he took off running again, the band now half a block away. Cheri turned left. The policeman just grinned.

It took nearly ten minutes for Cheri to make her way through traffic on Third Street. She parked in the grocery store parking lot, and walked rapidly toward First. There was Paul, standing on the corner next to Randy. The Weston High Marching Band was just passing by. Cheri ran the last half block and stopped breathless next to Paul. "You made it," he said with a big smile on his face.

"There he goes, Mom," Randy pointed up the street toward Chip.

Cheri caught a quick glance of her son before he was hidden behind the bass drums and the float that followed the band. "How did he look?" Cheri asked, trying to catch her breath.

"Chip was great," Randy replied, "and he was the only trumpet player who didn't have music clipped to his horn. He told me this morning he knows it all by heart."

"Or the music is still in the case on the back seat," Cheri replied.

"You obviously got him there on time," Paul commented as Cheri took hold of his arm.

Cheri looked up at Paul and grinned. "You might say that," she replied. "I'll tell you all about it. Or better yet . . . we should let Chip tell us all about it when he gets home."

"I think the parade is better this year than it was last year," Randy offered. "I just hope we beat the crap out of those East Chicago Mustangs!"

"Randy!" Cheri yelled, giving him the evil eye.

"Sorry, Mom," Randy replied, and carefully rephrased his words in a most serious tone, "I hope . . . we are victorious . . . in our game . . . against the Mustangs."

Paul stifled a laugh.

10

Cheri Walker had worked as the office manager at a
construction company in Twin Lakes, Wisconsin, before moving to Weston.
Their first son Chip was born a year after they were married, and Randy was
born less than two years later. She had enjoyed the bustling environment
in the construction office. Her job with a local law firm in Weston was even
more demanding, ordering supplies, paying bills, keeping track of billable
hours, salaries and paychecks, expense reimbursements and benefits.

It was not easy balancing the demands of job and family. She battled
feelings of resentment because Paul's work was so demanding, and often
took him away from the family in the evening. When the boys were younger,
he was good about being home when they came home from school. This
fall Chip was going into his junior year at Weston High School; and Randy,
their athlete, would be a sophomore.

Cheri had been the office manager for the growing firm of Etheridge,
Juarez, Fuscio, and Barkley for eight years. The law partners worked well
together and appreciated her efficient and professional leadership in the
office. Scott Etheridge, the senior partner and founder of the firm, was
affectionately called "the old man" by all of the partners, and he loved it.
Scott was in his mid-sixties and carried a large gut, over which his shirt
buttons continually strained. The knot in his tie was seldom seen, as it was
covered by his triple chin. He was no longer the first one to arrive at the
office in the morning, but he was usually the last one to leave at night.

The past few weeks had been extremely stressful for everyone in the firm.
Miguel Juarez was defending an illegal Mexican farm worker in a murder

trial. Miguel had done a lot of work for Mexicans immigrants, but this was the first involving a murder charge. Because of the illegal status, the case had been pro bono and required a lot of extra time from other staff members. Scott Etheridge, as senior partner, gave his support and advice as needed. Cheri, as office manager, had given Miguel all the encouragement she could muster. Last Friday, following hours of deliberation, the jury found the defendant "not guilty." However, because of his illegal status, he was immediately deported to Mexico.

The mood was bound to be lighter at the staff meeting this week. Cheri was surprised and a little curious about one small change. Scott asked her *not* to prepare an agenda this week. "I've got things pretty well in hand," he said, "and if anyone has anything else, they can bring it up under New Business." Cheri let it go at that.

Everyone gathered in the large conference room. Miguel Juarez was celebrating, and bought Mexican pastries to pass around. Scott Etheridge presided at the head of the long table and called the meeting to order. "Ladies and gentlemen . . ." Scott paused and waited for everyone's attention. "The first order of business today is to congratulate our colleague, Miguel Juarez, for his outstanding work on his recent case, and his hard-won victory on Friday." Everyone broke into applause, followed by several spontaneous shouts of "Congratulations!"

"The second order of business is somewhat related to the first," Scott continued, "and it gives me great pleasure. When I started this firm, I could see a need for someone familiar with the Latino community. Most of you know that Miguel was the first partner I took on as my case load grew. It seems appropriate, therefore, because of our history, and because of the trust and respect he has among all of you, that he becomes the next *Senior Partner.*" Scott paused.

"I've been calling him Señor Partner for years!" John Fuscio joked loudly. Everyone roared!

"But now you'll have to show me some respect, you dumb Dago!" Miguel joked in response.

The old man was enjoying the laughter as much as anyone, "All right, everyone, let's get serious. I've given this a lot of thought, and I think now is the time to recognize Miguel's contributions to our firm. That's why I want to make it official. As of today, Miguel Juarez is a Senior Partner."

"Congratulations, Miguel!" John Fuscio began the applause, and everyone joined him.

Miguel stood for a moment, bowing graciously. "I am most honored," Miguel replied. "I have to admit, I didn't see this coming, at least not this soon. Thank you Scott and I am most happy to accept the honor and the title."

The room quieted for the next item on Scott's agenda. "The third order of business is one that does not come easily for me." Scott paused again, and this time he looked at each partner in turn, focusing his gaze and smiling. Finally he spoke gravely, "After due consideration . . . and many prayerful conversations with my wife . . . . I have decided . . . to announce my retirement from the firm . . . as of September 1st this fall."

His words were followed by a long silence, with partners looking at each other, thoughts racing. Cheri could hardly believe it. A few people smiled bravely then quickly grew serious, as they realized how uncertain the future had just become. Glancing around the room, Scott grinned and spoke again, "C'mon guys, I'm not announcing my funeral, just my retirement!"

The tension in the air was broken and raucous laughter again filled the room. Shouts of "Congratulations!" were heard. Someone yelled, "It's about time, old man!" A scowl appeared on Scott's rugged face as he looked around the room to see who made the comment. Then he replied, "Maybe I was a bit hasty; perhaps I should reconsider." His scowl gradually became a grin and he broke into laughter again. As the room quieted, Scott continued.

"My wife and I would like to do a little traveling, and spend more time with the grandchildren. It just seems like a good time to step back and let you young folks take over. I leave, knowing the practice will continue under the capable leadership of Mr. Juarez, and that the office is in the good hands of Cheri Walker." He held out both hands toward Cheri.

Cheri got up and walked to his chair, leaned over and hugged him around the shoulders. "I'm gonna miss you," she whispered in his ear. "I'll miss you too," he said.

*   *   *

As Labor Day approached, Cheri's attention was on getting their sons ready for school. Their older son Chip, a junior, was excited about playing his trumpet in the marching band. Randy, a sophomore, was excited to be playing point guard on the junior varsity basketball team. Wednesday morning, as Cheri made the rounds in the office picking up billable hours and expense vouchers, Miguel Juarez reminded her about Scott's retirement luncheon at noon. "O my gosh," Cheri gasped, "I forgot to get a card . . . or order flowers . . . how could the luncheon slip my mind like that?"

Miguel smiled. "There's a card going around the office that everybody's signing. I think Evelyn has it." Cheri quickly returned to her desk, ordered flowers to be delivered to the restaurant, and went looking for Evelyn.

By October, Randy was at basketball practice after school every day; and Chip was practicing with the band. Each evening, after reading through the paper or watching the TV news, Cheri and Paul would talk about their work and the boys. "I've been thinking," Cheri mused aloud as she sipped the final drops of coffee from her mug. "These are important years for the boys and for us as parents. Chip and Randy are in high school and will soon be off to college. I've been thinking that with all the pressure I face at the law firm . . . maybe I should quit working for a while so I could be . . . you know, more available for Randy and Chip.

Paul listened intently, realizing a very significant discussion was about to take place. "Whew! I hardly know where to begin. The years certainly are flying by . . . and before we know it, Chip will be heading for college. But is this really the best time for you to quit working?"

"I know our two incomes have been really helpful, but I wonder . . . if . . . maybe right now . . . our time isn't more important than the money."

"That's a good point, Cher. I know I hate to miss Randy's games because of church conflicts. You know I try to make it to all the boy's activities unless there's an emergency."

"I know, honey, you're a great dad . . . and the boys really look up to you. They understand the importance of your work as a pastor. And I wouldn't want you to give that up. Maybe I'm being selfish, but I've been at the law firm for eight years, and I really feel like I could use a break."

"Does old man Etheridge's retirement have anything to do with it?"

"Not really . . . well, maybe . . . not exactly, I mean, it just got me to thinking about the freedom he is enjoying now. Then I thought how much I would enjoy some freedom in my life."

"I just heard the phone in the kitchen;" Paul interrupted, "I'll grab it." Paul walked quickly to the kitchen. "Hello . . . Yes, this is Pastor Walker . . . Oh, no, I'm so sorry to hear that . . . Yes, I'll be there in ten or fifteen minutes."

"Who was that, honey?"

"It was a nurse from the emergency room at the hospital. Darrel's wife, Francine, just had a heart attack. He asked the nurse to call me."

"I can't say I ever get used to you running for emergencies. I'm sure Darrel will appreciate your coming, but think about what I've proposed. We can finish our discussion another time."

At the hospital Paul walked quickly through the hall to the E.R. and was greeted by a very distraught Darrel Thomas. "Thank you so much for coming, Pastor. Francine was fixing dinner in the kitchen. All of a sudden I heard a pot clang on the floor, and when I got to the kitchen, there she was, passed out on the floor."

"So sorry, Darrel, I'm so sorry. Has the doctor said anything about her prognosis?"

"It doesn't look good, Pastor. They've got her hooked up to life support, but they said her heart had stopped for several minutes, and it's not beating on its own." Darrel began sobbing. Paul wrapped his arm around his shoulder and held him.

After a minute, Darrel calmed and drew back. "Pastor, what am I gonna do?"

At that moment, the doctor came out of the examining room and walked over to them. Darrel introduced him, "Doctor, this is my pastor, Paul Walker, from the Lutheran church."

"Good to meet you, sir; nice of you to come. Mr. Thomas, I'm afraid I have some very bad news. We've just finished an EEG which measures brain activity, and . . ." the doctor shook his head, "there is no sign of brain function."

"What does that mean?" Darrel asked, fear in his eyes.

"Basically, it means she is gone, and we won't be able to bring her back."

Darrel began sobbing. Tears of compassion streamed from Paul's eyes. A few minutes later Darrel stepped into the examining room to see his wife one more time. He sobbed again as he laid his head on her chest and wrapped his arms around her.

*   *   *

Francine's funeral was held at Trinity the following Saturday. The women's circle to which she belonged put on a fabulous luncheon. Darrel moved quietly among the mourners, greeting and thanking them. Each shared a special memory of Francine. Several church members commented to Paul about how difficult it would be, since Darrel and Francine had not had any children. The women in the kitchen whispered quietly, "He's going to be SO alone." "What will he do without Francine?"

That evening Paul and Cheri sat in their living room talking about Francine, and Darrel, and the funeral. Paul said, "Remember about a week ago when you were talking about how fast the years are flying? You said something I've been thinking about . . . a lot."

"What's that?"

"You said maybe our time is more important than money. Remember?"

"I sure do," Cheri replied.

"The events of this week have confirmed that, in a way that leaves no doubt in my mind." Paul paused to reflect on the funeral and Francine's sudden cardiac arrest. "Cheri, you are so precious . . . to me . . . and to the boys. If you want to retire from the law firm, why don't you do it?"

"Oh, Paul . . ." Cheri moved next to him on the sofa and gave him a big hug.

"Does this mean you've made a decision?" Paul asked.

Cheri smiled, revealing the dimples that Paul just loved, and nodded a yes. "I've been thinking I might work through the end of the year and turn in my resignation in January. Then, maybe we can plan that trip to the Holy Land we've always talked about."

"Whatever you decide is fine with me," Paul answered.

11

Kathy Stiletto was so pleased she had captured the quarterback's heart that she never gave another thought to Michael Greenwood. She had, however, been thinking about Trinity Lutheran Church where she had attended Brian Holloway's memorial. Now that Kevin had actually proposed, she fell asleep each night thinking what a beautiful wedding it would be in that lovely old church with the stained-glass windows. She had made plans for the reception at a local hall, the musicians, the flowers, the cake, and her wedding gown. All that was left was to call the church to arrange for the wedding service.

It was the end of November. Paul felt energized, looking forward to Christmas, and his wife's retirement soon thereafter. Next Sunday would be the first Sunday in Advent. He had just spoken on the phone with the chair of the Altar Guild about the blue paraments for the altar and pulpit, the placing of the Advent wreath and candles, and the special banner to be hung in the chancel. Paul had always enjoyed Advent, a season of hope, expectation, and preparation for the coming of the Messiah, Israel's king. He felt badly that many young people don't understand why the church marks these four Sundays before Christmas with special colors and symbols and Advent candles. At this time of year, Christianity and Judaism are especially close. Christians wait for Christ's return as Jews wait for the Messiah. Christians borrow language and images from the Old Testament, the Jewish scriptures, to link the past and future.

"Pastor, call for you on line 1," Carol announced.

"Good morning, this is Pastor Paul."

"Hi, my name is Kathy and I wanted to talk to someone about our wedding."

"Hi, Kathy. I'd be happy to make an appointment with you and your fiancé."

"Oh, cool! Kevin and I want a Christmas wedding. How soon can we meet?"

"Wow! That's short notice, but why don't you come to my office and we'll see what we can do? Can we meet tomorrow night?"

"That would be great! I'll tell Kevin. What time should we come?"

"Is seven thirty okay with you?"

"We'll be there. Thanks, Pastor!"

Paul jotted the names on his calendar, leaned back and reflected. *Just what I need, a Christmas wedding! I don't think Kathy is a member of the church, so few of my weddings are these days.*

The next evening, Paul tried to clear some items from his desk as he waited for . . . he glanced at his desk calendar to remember the names . . . Kathy and Kevin. At seven forty-five he heard the buzzer at the parking lot door. He decided to go to the door rather than using the office button to unlock the door.

"Welcome to Trinity! I'm Pastor Paul Walker."

"Hi! I'm Kathy, Kathy Stiletto, like in high heels. And this is my fiancé, Kevin Gianopoulis." They shook hands and Paul led them upstairs to the office.

"Congratulations! I'll bet you're both excited about the wedding," Paul said, as he offered chairs for the young couple.

"Oh, it's gonna be so beautiful! I can hardly wait!" bubbled Kathy.

"I'm looking forward to getting acquainted," Paul said, "but first, let me ask what date you had in mind for the wedding."

"Saturday, December 21st, right before Christmas. I know that's a busy time, but I've always dreamed of a Christmas wedding!"

"Well, I usually like to meet with couples three or four times before a wedding to do some pre-marital counseling. Are you willing to do that?"

"Sure!" Kathy replied. Paul glanced at Kevin who, up to this point, had not said a word. Kathy turned to Kevin and pulled on his sleeve. "We can do that; no problem, right?"

"Yeah . . . I guess so," Kevin shrugged.

"Tell me a little about yourselves," Paul suggested. "How long have you been going together?"

"We met at Weston High School about three years ago, at the end of our junior year. Kevin was the quarterback for the varsity team."

"Yeah, senior year we went twelve and one," Kevin interjected.

"Kevin jokes about how he used to call the plays, but now I give the orders," Kathy added, looking at Kevin with a grin.

"And what made you choose Trinity for your wedding?" Paul asked the couple.

"Well, we came to Brian Holloway's memorial service that summer after graduation," Kathy answered. "That was really a sad day."

"Yes, it was," Paul agreed. "We all miss Brian very much around here."

"That was the first time I'd ever been inside a Lutheran church," Kathy continued again. "It felt so holy in here. Really awesome! I remember thinking to myself, if I ever get married, this is the kind of church I'd like to have."

Paul smiled. "And now, here you are; but this time, for a much happier occasion."

"Right. And I'm so excited about our wedding. I've got a reception hall reserved, and the caterers! My best friend works in a flower shop, and she's going to be my maid of honor! Kevin's excited too, aren't you, honey."

"Well, sure. A bunch of guys from high school, my former teammates are gonna be my . . . my . . . what do you call them?" he asked, looking at Kathy.

"Groomsmen, silly. Anyway, our colors are red and green, like Christmas, right? The bridesmaids will all wear green satin dresses and carry red carnations. I'll be in white of course, with a bouquet of red roses. So, what I was wondering Pastor, you know those banner thingies on the altar and podium? I'd like the color on the altar to be green, and the one on the podium to be red. Is that okay?"

"Well, Kathy, let me explain, those 'thingies' are called paraments. They set the theme for each season of the church year, white for special holy days, purple represents royalty for Lent, and blue represents hope for Advent. You can't have two different colors in the church at the same time. Not only that, but we don't change the paraments for weddings."

"Oh, Pastor, just this once?" Kathy begged sweetly. "Blue will look just dreadful with green and red!" Kathy began to pout.

"I'm sorry, but if I did it for you, I'd have to do it for every bride. The church tradition is clear. The color for Advent is blue."

"That's the trouble with the church!" Kathy declared angrily. "There's no flexibility! I can't believe it!" Kathy ranted on. "Can you imagine our wedding pictures, how awful they'll look with blue PARAMENTS behind the green dresses?" She nearly spit the word "paraments."

"Kathy, honey," Kevin interjected, "I told you we shouldn't get married in a church."

"But, Kevin, this church is so beautiful! It's what I've always dreamed about!"

A long silence followed as Kathy tried to calm down. Paul tried not to say anything that would make the situation worse. Again, he was reminded why he was so reluctant to do weddings for couples who were not part of the church community. On the other hand, it was an opportunity to talk with them about God and the sacredness of marriage. Kathy seemed to be thinking, possibly having a change of heart. Paul waited.

"Look, Pastor, my parents are quite wealthy. Let's say we could make a very large gift to you or your church if you make a small exception." Paul could hardly believe what he was hearing. "The wedding is on Saturday, right? And none of your members will be here until Sunday, right? So, who's gonna know? I'm thinking maybe . . . five hundred dollars would be a nice honorarium for the pastor. What do you think?" Kathy leaned toward Paul smiling her most seductive smile.

Five hundred dollars? the first thing that came to Paul's mind was how they could use the money for a trip to the Holy Land. *No! It's not right. It's a bribe, pure and simple. And I would never accept a bribe.* Paul struggled to shape an answer to Kathy. *Paraments? What's the big deal? It's a symbolic thing, meaningful to church members, but obviously without any sacred meaning to this self-centered young woman. Would it do any harm to have green paraments on the altar for one day? Of course not. But it's the principle.*

Kathy smiled. The longer the pastor thought about it, the more confident she was of her victory. Paul replied, "Kathy, I can't accept a bribe. Why don't you let me think about this? Maybe we can come up with a solution. Let's meet again next week. If we can't reach an agreement at our next meeting, you can make other arrangements. Are you willing to give this more thought? You and Kevin discuss the situation and let me know if you want to change your plans."

"Sure, Pastor. Let's meet again next week. I know we can work something out."

Paul asked the couple to fill out a Wedding Information Sheet, with the date of the rehearsal, the wedding, and contact numbers for the bride and groom. He also handed them a brochure, "Guidelines for Weddings at Trinity." After a few more pleasantries, the couple left his office.

Paul breathed a sigh of relief, locked the church offices, and drove home. He prayed for Kevin and Kathy, and for wisdom to know how to handle this frustrating situation.

Throughout his busy week, Paul struggled with conflicted feelings about Kathy and Kevin. *Altar paraments are not as important as people. Maybe Kathy was right; the church is too stuck in its medieval traditions. Maybe I was being inflexible. Maybe the blue paraments aren't important.*

A few hours later, Paul found himself arguing the other side of the coin. *Is it right for the church to abandon its principles just to please a generation of people who want everything on their terms? Today's young people are so accustomed to having their way they have no respect for the experience or wisdom of their elders. My way or the highway is their motto. I don't care how important the color scheme is to dear Kathy, there are other things that are more important! Does God mean anything to them or not?*

When Kevin and Kathy returned the following week, Paul had a compromise in mind. He felt certain he was being flexible. He was pretty sure Kathy would buy it. If she did, they could move on to more important matters.

"Hey, Pastor Paul!" Kathy greeted him as she and Kevin came into the office.

"Hey, Kathy! Hey, Kevin!" Paul replied. "Have a seat."

"I read that brochure you gave us last week," Kathy began.

"Do you have any questions?" Paul asked.

"No, not really. I was just wondering if you've decided about those banners on the altar and podium."

"Well, Kathy, I've given it a lot of thought. I hope you have too. Are you willing to leave the blue paraments on for the wedding?"

"Absolutely not! I told you last week . . . that would look terrible!"

"And I'm not willing to put the wrong color on the altar." Paul waited a moment. "But I have a proposal that I hope we both can agree on." He hesitated again to watch her reaction. "Since the altar and pulpit, and all the wood arches are white, why don't we take the paraments off the altar and the pulpit and leave them bare? Would that work for you?"

Kathy rolled her eyes, sighed, and looked out the window.

Kevin wanted desperately to get this over with. "Sounds like a pretty good idea to me."

Kathy shook her head. "Men never understand. Too bad this church doesn't have a woman pastor. Women understand about weddings."

"I don't think that's the issue," Paul argued.

"Just forget it! C'mon Kevin. We don't have to take this nonsense!" Kathy rose to leave.

"But the pastor just said he would compromise," Kevin begged.

She yanked on his shirt sleeve to pull him out of his seat. "I've already made other arrangements. The reception hall will let us decorate ANY WAY WE WANT. My bridesmaid, Andrea, told me HER PASTOR would even come to the hall to do the wedding. C'mon Kevin." At the office door, Kathy turned and faced Paul. With her most pathetic voice she sneered, "I really wanted to be married at Trinity, but you blew it. I hope you're happy!" She turned again and disappeared down the hall.

Paul sat in the empty office stunned. *I blew it? I blew it? I was being reasonable. Good luck, Kevin. I hope you know what you're getting into.*

As Paul drove home, reflecting on the encounters, both last week and tonight, he was finally blessed with a great sense of relief. Then he even started to laugh. *A Christmas wedding! I can do without that!* Paul laughed to himself all the way home. *Kathy Stiletto! Sorry, Kathy, no wedding bells at Trinity . . . . . All because we have the wrong colored thingies!*

12

A trip to the Holy Land, Paul and Cheri
had been talking about it for several months. Discussion about it was
put on hold due to the Christmas holiday and Cheri's much-anticipated
retirement. On the first working day of January Cheri submitted her
resignation to Miguel Juarez. Though it saddened everyone to hear she
would be leaving, Cheri's resignation was graciously accepted by the
law firm. She had worked for several months after Scott Etheridge's
retirement to make sure everything was running smoothly. She agreed
to help orient the new office manager the last week in January.

Meanwhile, Paul was battling New Year fatigue, church issues, and feelings
of depression. He was accustomed to a post-Christmas let-down, but this
year seemed worse than usual. The disastrous meetings with Kathy and
Kevin were still troubling him. He was worried about Reiner Holtz who
seemed to be getting more paranoid. He was struggling with his annual
report to the congregation that would be presented at the annual meeting
the first Sunday in February. In spite of a strong Christmas offering, the
congregation had fallen short of the projected income for the year. He
wondered what church members would think about their trip to the Holy
Land at a time when church finances were down.

One evening after dinner, Paul and Cheri were watching the evening
news on television. The reporter was talking about crime in Chicago. Paul
suddenly grabbed the remote and hit OFF. He sat in his favorite chair,
staring at the dark TV screen.

"What's the matter?" Cheri asked.

"I don't know," Paul confessed. "I've just been feeling really down lately. I feel like I've hit a crisis point in my preaching. I don't know if *I* believe what I'm saying to others."

"Paul, you know you tend to be hard on yourself. I think your sermons sound as confident as ever. And there is a depth of compassion which I think is more evident than ever before."

"I've been thinking about that incident with Kathy Stiletto, right before Christmas. I truly want to work with the younger generation, but some of them are just so . . . so . . . I don't know . . . They think they can have everything their way."

"Isn't that why some people call them the *entitlement generation?*" Cheri reflected.

"You know what else is troubling me?" Paul asked beseechingly.

"No, what else is troubling you?"

"You know the Holtz's who joined the church last fall?"

"Yes, but I haven't visited with them much; so I can't say I know them very well."

Paul let out a deep sigh. "I can't stop thinking about my visits at their home. Reiner has a very unique family history. He said some really weird things. He even talked about a conspiracy theory which he apparently thinks is valid. At church recently, his eyes seem more nervous than ever. I'm worried about him."

"That's why I think it would be good for us to get away for a while. You've just got too much on your mind."

"That's another thing;" Paul reflected, "I've been misplacing reminder notes all year long. Maybe I'm getting senile . . . or losing my mind."

"It's just the stress. Believe me; there have been days at the law office when I thought I was losing my mind." Cheri rose from her chair, stepped over to Paul, reached down and gave him a hug. But Paul didn't respond and didn't look up. He was on a roll and ready to pour it all out.

"Maybe the cynics are right; the world really is going to hell and everyone is too damn selfish to do anything about it. Maybe the agnostics are right; no one really knows anything about God; it's all just blind faith. Maybe the scientists are right; the only things we know for certain are things we can measure and test for reliability. It feels like everything I say in my sermons on Sunday morning is wishful thinking. I hope this, and I pray for that, and may blessings be yours, and this is what Jesus did, even if it is hard to believe . . . . And believe me, *I'm finding it hard to believe.*"

"Paul, that's just not like you. You've always had a healthy skepticism, but the way you're talking now is starting to worry me. I really think it would do you a world of good to see the Holy Land. You've always said you'd like to actually set foot on the same paths Jesus walked."

"That's true, Cheri. But a trip like that costs a small fortune."

"I know, I know. But let me ask you, what better use could there be for the money we inherited from my folks? That money is just sitting there in the bank, not doing anyone any good. I think my parents would love to know we've used it to fulfill a dream of ours. We can celebrate my retirement AND give us both something to look forward to."

"Oh, Cher, maybe you're right. Everything else in the world may be screwed up, but at least I've got you . . . . Maybe we should get away for a while . . . . Anyway, thanks for listening. I love you so much."

"Love you too. Promise me, tomorrow you'll call Global Travel and make the arrangements."

"I promise."

*   *   *

Cheri spent her last day at work celebrating and saying her good-byes. Miguel Juarez told her if she ever needed legal counsel to give him a call. Little did either of them realize at the time, how significant an offer it would turn out to be.

The first Monday morning in February Cheri woke up with the alarm, helped see Chip and Randy off to school and Paul off to work. She poured herself a second cup of coffee and sat down at the kitchen table. She suddenly felt lost and alone, uncertain of why she felt so weird, and uncertain of what she should do next. "I'm free!" she finally said aloud. "I don't have to go to work today." The strange disoriented feeling turned to elation. "I'm free!" She shouted to God and the world, "I'M FREE! AND WE'RE GOING TO ISRAEL!"

13

Call Global Travel. Paul put the note on
the corner of the desk. He thought before calling he would talk to his
friend Ryan Jacoby, the pastor at the Methodist church. Ryan and his wife
had been to Israel. He might have some suggestions of what to see and
what to avoid. It might take some searching on line to make their plane
reservations or find special packages for the Holy Land. He wanted at least
a ballpark figure of how much it would cost before meeting with the travel
agent. Cheri had agreed traveling the last two weeks in February would
allow a month for planning, and would be a perfect time to get away.

Fred Schmidt showed up at the church office at 11:45. "You got any plans
for lunch, Pastor?"

Paul glanced at his calendar and replied, "Nope! Let's go!" After ordering
their favorite soup and salad, Paul began sharing his excitement about
going to the Middle East.

"Never been there," responded Fred, "but I think pastors would find it most
interesting."

"There's just so much history there. And to see the actual towns and
mountains and valleys where Jesus walked and preached and healed has
got to make it even more real than just reading about it," Paul affirmed.

That afternoon, after talking with Ryan Jacoby, he called Global Travel and
made an appointment for the next morning. He forgot all about the note
on his desk which had mysteriously disappeared. He was just so excited

to tell Cheri about what he had learned from Ryan and to confirm the proposed dates in February.

*   *   *

A week later Liz, the treasurer, heard the announcement at church about the pastor's trip to the Holy Land. She remembered the note she had found on the pastor's desk: Call Global Travel. Slowly, a most marvelous plan began to take shape in her mind.

One evening after work she presented part of her plan, just part of it, to her husband. "Phillip, I've been thinking. We haven't taken a really great vacation together for a long time. Remember the wonderful time we had in Bermuda on our honeymoon? That was so long ago. We've both been working extremely hard lately, and I think we deserve some time away."

"It has been a long time since we've traveled together. And you're right about our jobs. Did you have something specific in mind?"

"Well, now that you mention it, I've been putting some money away in a special secret account. I was thinking either the Mediterranean, or Australia and New Zealand."

"Australia? Hmm . . . I've always wanted to see kangaroos up close and personal," Phil replied, smiling. "The only hard part will be scheduling a mutual break in our jobs."

"I've thought about that too. I've worked with Paulette on several big sales, and I think she could handle the closings if I were gone. Maybe we could get away from the bitter cold we're bound to have in March. Haven't things slowed down a little for you this winter?"

"I suppose I could schedule my subcontractors to be working while I escape for a week or two."

"Then let's do it!" Liz nearly shouted as she reached out to hug her husband.

*　　*　　*

The next day Liz began researching a trip to Australia and the Great Barrier Reef. She discovered that it was summer "down under," and they would be far from the cold winter days of Indiana. She phoned Global Travel and set up an appointment to discuss their travel arrangements. Liz reached into her purse and pulled out the checkbook for the Pastor's Discretionary Fund. She made a check payable to Global Travel and left the amount blank. Then she opened the file from the Walker's home purchase and carefully copied Paul's signature onto the check.

A couple of days later, after discussing some of the details of the trip with Phil, she stopped in the office of Global Travel on her lunch break. The trip for Phillip and herself was scheduled for the first three weeks in March. The travel agent printed the agenda for their trip and a sheet with the costs for reservations which had to be paid up front. Liz fumbled through her purse and pretended she had forgotten her checkbook. She promised a check for the reservations would be in the mail the next day. She hoped she wouldn't have to answer any questions about the check from the Discretionary Fund.

*　　*　　*

Preparations for both the Walkers and the Sterlings went smoothly. Both couples were blessed with wonderful trips! Paul and Cheri couldn't believe the contrasts they saw in Israel. Tel Aviv was a modern city in so many ways, and yet, within a short bus ride into the dry, barren countryside, Paul felt transported into biblical times. The city of Jerusalem was filled with ancient sights and sites. There really was a rabbi named Jesus of Nazareth, who had been crucified in Jerusalem. It was easier, now, to see Him on the mountain, breaking the loaves and feeding five thousand. The Jordan River, where Jesus was baptized, was vividly real. Paul could now picture Jesus getting into a fishing boat on the Sea of Galilee with his disciples.

He and Cheri talked about their faith and their family. They reminisced about how God had led them into marriage, blessed them with two fine sons, and led them from Twin Lakes, Wisconsin, to Indiana, and now to the Holy Land. They returned to Weston tired, yet refreshed and renewed.

Phillip and Liz returned to Weston three weeks later, delighted with their vacation. They had enjoyed the glamorous hotel in Sidney and the sights of Sidney harbor. Phil was thrilled with the jeep tour through the outback where they saw kangaroos and koalas. Liz's favorite was the boat tour of the Barrier Reef and the beautiful mountains and waterfalls of New Zealand.

One always wishes the glow of a special event would last longer than it does. Paul returned to his routines at church the first of March. Cheri remained giddy a bit longer, with time at home to reflect on all they had witnessed and learned. She busied herself organizing and captioning their photos, and sending souvenirs to Chip and Randy.

A few weeks later, Liz showed up at the church with a tan she had gotten while sun-bathing poolside at their hotel in Sidney. Phillip returned to his office at Sterling Homes and began dealing with sub-contractors, mistakes, and delays at the construction site.

The rest of Liz's plan, accusing the pastor of embezzlement, could wait until later. *It might be good,* she thought, *to work out the details very carefully.*

14

Carlos Arriaga's brother, Juan, was only 19 when he was gunned down in Nogales, Mexico. He and his friends had visas to work a construction job in Tucson. Early in the morning they gathered near the border crossing, waiting for one more companion. A car drove up and made a quick U-turn, throwing up a cloud of dust as it veered onto the shoulder and stopped perpendicular to the dotted lane marker. Two gunmen jumped out of the back seat and began firing into the small group of construction workers, killing Juan Arriaga and three others. Two workers were wounded but survived.

Nogales police believe the killing was gang related, and ordered by drug lord Vincente Carrillo Fuentes. Police suspected La Linea had executed the workers. Carlos did not know which of his brother's friends was involved in drug trafficking, but he knew his brother Juan was an innocent victim of the violence. "Too many innocent victims!" he cried when officers told him of his brother's death.

On the day of the funeral mass, Carlos sat in church with his wife Lolita and parents, and he sobbed. At the graveside, when the committal ended, he screamed again, "Too many . . . innocent . . . victims!"

Carlos and Lolita were tired of the cartel wars, and would do anything to keep their children safe. Rosa was three when Juan was killed, and her little brother was born a month later. Little Juan was named after Carlos' brother. The Arriagas hoped to be approved for emigration to the United States. Several years passed before their visa was approved. They were assigned to *Lutheran Immigration and Refugee Service* and told they would be received by a sponsoring congregation as soon as one was found.

Attorney Miguel Juarez had shared much of his work with Cheri during the time she worked at the law firm. The stories he told gave Cheri a different perspective on both legal and illegal immigrants. She could not help but share some of the more tragic stories with Paul. When the LIRS newsletter asked Lutheran congregations to sponsor immigrant families, Paul saw another opportunity for ministry. He called the LIRS office in Baltimore, Maryland, to express interest and was told about the Arriaga family and their need for a sponsoring congregation.

An immigration committee was quickly formed. Cheri, recently retired, had some time available, and felt a passion for this new ministry. Darrel Thomas was no longer on the council or Building and Property Committee because his term had expired. Since his wife Francine's passing, he felt his life was pretty aimless. He was looking for something new and volunteered for the new committee. They were joined by Maria Olivera, who was excited to help a Latino family, and Chuck Kushman, who had served for many years as head usher. At their first meeting, Darrel was nominated to chair the committee and graciously accepted. Cheri read the letter Paul had received from the Lutheran Immigration Service which told the background of the Arriagas and their children. Cheri also offered to call Miguel Juarez at the law office to ask if he would provide legal counsel to their committee.

Maria responded to the letter by telling the story of how she had come to Texas with her husband to work in the fields on temporary visas. "We applied for permanent residence and it was finally granted." Maria looked up to heaven and cried, "Madre de Dios, why?"

The committee members looked at her in shock. They expected her to look happy, but her face appeared anguished. She continued, "The week after we were granted permanent resident status, my husband was killed in a car accident."

This was the first time Maria has spoken to members of Trinity about her husband. "It was so many years ago . . . so many years. I pray to Mary that God will smile more favorably on Carlos and Lolita."

Cheri reached across the table and grasped Maria's hands. The first meeting closed with prayers for Maria, and for Carlos Arriaga, his wife Lolita and their children, Rosa and Juan.

*   *   *

"Hello, Cheri, I'm delighted you called. We've missed you around here." It was good to hear Miguel's voice again.

"I miss all of you, too, but I'm enjoying my retirement," Cheri responded.

"What can I do for you?"

"Remember you told me to call if I needed any legal advice?" Cheri asked.

"Yes, I remember, but I hope neither you nor Paul is in any kind of legal trouble."

"No, no, nothing like that, thank goodness. But I do want to ask a favor."

"Go ahead. I'll do what I can."

"Our congregation has decided to sponsor an immigrant family from Mexico."

"Wonderful! Wonderful!" Miguel replied enthusiastically. "What can I do to help?"

"Carlos Arriaga and his family will be arriving in Chicago in ten days. Chuck Kushman has a large van and he has agreed to meet them at O'Hare and bring them with all their belongings down here to Weston."

"Congratulations to the Arriagas! They couldn't ask for better sponsors! I look forward to meeting them. You may not know this, but I've helped our local parish resettle several Hispanic families. Father Muldoon thinks I'm an expert. I'll be happy to sit down with them and complete the necessary paper work for the Immigration and Naturalization Service."

"Thank you, thank you!" Cheri was jubilant. "I was hoping you would do that for us."

"No problem, Cheri, I'm glad to be of assistance to the church as well as the Arriaga family."

"You're a good Catholic, Miguel. Any chance we can talk you into becoming a Lutheran?"

"Thanks, but no thanks," Miguel replied.

Several weeks later, on a beautiful April morning, the Arriaga family made their first appearance at church. They were introduced by Darrel Thomas and received a rousing round of applause. Carlos introduced his wife Lolita and his two children, both of whom spoke excellent English which they had learned at school in Nogales. The one member who didn't applaud was Reiner Holtz. His wife clapped timidly until she noticed Reiner was not clapping, so she stopped. No one noticed Reiner's scowl, or if they did, they ignored it.

Pastor Walker gave a brief welcome and invited the congregation to meet and visit with the Arriagas during the coffee hour reception in their honor.

In the weeks that followed, Cheri kept Paul informed about the progress made in settling the Arriagas in their new home and city. They began attending mass at St. Mary's Catholic Church, which generated a lively discussion among the members of the Immigration Committee. Chuck Kushman was miffed. "Seems to me, they should be joining Trinity since we're their sponsoring church."

Maria Olivera couldn't understand where Chuck was coming from. Didn't he know Catholics aren't supposed to go to any other church?

"You'd think they'd be grateful for all we've done," Chuck continued. "Why would they leave us and start going to St. Mary's?"

Maria felt she had to explain, "For those who are raised Catholic, especially in Mexico, to attend any other church was forbidden. I remember how I felt when I first came to Trinity. I appreciated the reward I received, and I appreciated the warm friendship extended to me by Mrs. Walker and many other members of the church. At first, I thought Trinity was too informal, like it wasn't a REAL church. For me, being a Catholic, I was used to a feeling of mystery and holiness, you know, with statues of Mary and Jesus all around. Thank goodness for that beautiful statue of Jesus behind the altar here at Trinity. When I first came to mass here I kept my eyes on Him, asking Him if it was all right for me to be in this church. Then I found that the Lutheran church has the sacrament; but it isn't called Mass; and Pastor Paul gives us both the body and the blood. In Mexico we only received the body of our Lord. And baptisms are the same. And everyone here prays most humbly. And finally, after many months, I felt like Trinity was a real church too! But I can understand why Carlos and Lolita want to take their children to St. Mary's."

As chair of the committee, Darrel Thomas hesitated to comment too soon.

Cheri spoke up. "Maria is right. The Lutheran church is proud to sponsor immigrants, and we want them to feel welcome in our church; but there is no rule that says they must join the sponsoring congregation."

"I guess I see your point." Chuck seemed willing to give up his expectation.

"Then I think our mission is clear," summarized Darrel, "we will continue working to help Carlos find a job, and Lolita to learn English, and to get the children settled in school. And we won't make them feel guilty about not coming to Trinity. Agreed?"

"Agreed," everyone responded.

Cheri was pleased to tell Paul that Carlos had been hired at the local paint manufacturing plant in Weston. Juan and Rosa were enrolled in second and fourth grade. Lolita enrolled in an evening *English as Second Language* class at Weston High. With the aid of her daughter Rosa as interpreter, Lolita reported that she had enjoyed her first grocery shopping adventure at the local supermarket. Lolita also shared that she was making friends at St. Mary's. Some of the parents she met there also had children in the same public school as Rosa and Juan.

In the months that followed, Carlos and Lolita became more and more independent. The Immigration Committee met less and less frequently, and finally agreed that the experience was like raising kids, who at some point, had to be given their independence. Miguel Juarez was a tremendous help in filling out citizenship applications. The committee agreed they were definitely committed to sponsoring another family, perhaps in another year or two.

15

Reiner Holtz was not impressed with the dark-skinned Mexicans whom Trinity members seemed so happy to welcome. He could understand the migrant workers in Texas and California, but why did they have to come all the way to Indiana? And why was the government allowing them to settle as permanent residents? Liz Sterling saw the whole project as another one of Paul Walker's popularity ploys. *Welcome the aliens! Another new ministry! It makes me sick.* She would find the immigrants a cheap rental from among her listings, but it gave her one more reason to resent the young pastor. One of these days she would finish her lovely scheme.

The Arriaga family had been an exciting lift for Paul and Cheri. Trinity members seemed excited about welcoming the newcomers to the United States and to Weston. On Tuesday morning, following the reception, Paul received a phone call from the attorney, Miguel Juarez. "Good morning, Pastor, how are you?"

"Fine, thank you, Miguel. We had a great day at church Sunday introducing the Arriaga family. And by the way, thanks again for offering your help with their papers."

"Ah, no problem, Pastor; I'm glad to help." Miguel paused.

"Is there something on your mind, Miguel?" Paul asked. Usually it was Paul or Cheri who called Miguel. This morning, Miguel had initiated the contact.

"Well, Pastor, I hate to trouble you."

"No, no. I owe you big time for all you've done for our church. What can I do for you?"

"I'm not sure what to make of it, but I had a strange phone call yesterday afternoon."

Paul waited a moment for Miguel to continue. Finally he asked, "What made it strange?"

"Someone called but would not identify himself. It was a man with a German accent. He said, 'We're on to you. I know about your plan . . . .'"

"What plan?" Paul asked.

"That's exactly what I asked him," Miguel continued. "Your plan to help the Mexicans, he said."

"Did he say anything else?"

"I'm afraid so. He also said, and I quote, 'You and Pastor Walker are making a big mistake. Just consider yourselves warned.' Then he hung up."

"That doesn't sound good. Do you have any idea who it might have been?"

"None whatsoever . . . I was hoping, since he mentioned your name that you might know who it was. Could it be a member of Trinity?"

"I suppose that's possible. You said he had a German accent?"

"Yes; it was quite distinctive."

"I have a hunch who it might be. But before I say his name, let me give it some more thought. I certainly don't like the threatening tone of his warning."

"He certainly made me uncomfortable, Pastor. I really felt you ought to know about this. There are laws against threatening someone, you know."

"I appreciate your informing me, Miguel. If it's the person I think it is, I don't think he's dangerous, just a little delusional perhaps."

"Let me know what you decide. Please don't take any unnecessary chances. And I'll let you know if I get any more calls from him."

"Thanks, Miguel. We'll talk again soon."

"Thank you, Pastor."

That evening, Paul decided to talk with Cheri about the call from Miguel Juarez. Her reaction was instantaneous, "It's got to be that crazy Reiner Holtz!"

"What makes you so sure?"

"Who else in our congregation has a thick German accent? And who talks about *plans and conspiracies*? Hmm?" Cheri tipped her head and gave him a knowing smile.

"Well, to be honest, Reiner was the only person who came to my mind also. Has he said anything to you or any members of your Immigration Committee?"

"Not that I'm aware of," Cheri answered.

"I've been thinking I might give Reiner a call."

"He'll probably get defensive."

"I'll try to keep it low key . . . ask how he's doing . . . just let him talk." Paul was struggling for direction and encouragement, and he trusted Cheri's judgment.

"I suppose it wouldn't hurt." Cheri reflected. "You are his pastor, and you have a right to be concerned."

Half an hour later, Paul went into the study, closed the door, and dialed Reiner's number.

"Hello?" a timid voice answered.

"Hello, Tillie, this is Pastor Walker calling. Is Reiner home?"

"No . . . ." she answered softly.

"Do you expect him back this evening?" Paul inquired.

"No . . . . I don't think so." Again, she seemed hesitant to talk.

Paul was growing more and more uncomfortable. He didn't want to pressure Tillie, nor intrude on their privacy, but he really wanted to talk with Reiner. "When do you expect him?"

"I . . . I don't know," Tillie's voice quavered.

"Tillie, is something wrong with you or Reiner?" Paul felt it was time to push a little deeper.

"I . . . I . . . I don't know." Tillie hesitated. "I don't know what's wrong, but I'm worried about Reiner."

"When did you last see him?" Paul asked.

"Sunday evening. Pastor, I don't know if I should tell you, but Reiner was very upset Sunday."

"What seemed to be the matter, Tillie?"

"I think it was that Mexican family at church Sunday morning. Reiner didn't seem very pleased to see them. You know he has a thing about Mexicans."

"Yes, Tillie, I'm aware of his concerns. He feels, as do many Americans, that too many Mexicans are being allowed into the United States." Paul didn't hold this opinion, but he thought acknowledging it might put Tillie more at ease talking about Reiner.

"Oh, Pastor, I'm afraid it's worse than that. Reiner grumbled and grumbled all afternoon about Mexicans taking over our country. Then, after supper, he gave me a kiss and said goodbye. He said not to worry; he had a lot of work to do. He took his laptop computer with him. He said he might be gone a few days, but he didn't tell me where he was going."

"He left Sunday evening and he hasn't come back yet? Has he called?"

"No, Pastor. He hasn't called or come home. I'm getting worried."

"Oh, Tillie, I'm sorry to hear that. Do you have any idea where he might have gone?"

"No. No, I can't think straight. I HAVE NO CLUE! Is that the expression?"

Paul laughed. Tillie's sense of humor relieved the tension, his and hers. "Do you need someone to come and stay with you?" Paul asked. "I could call someone."

"Oh, no, no. I couldn't think of it. Reiner would be furious if he found out someone stayed in our house. I'll be fine, Pastor."

"Okay. But you call me or Cheri if you need anything, or if you change your mind. And if Reiner comes home, please tell him I'd like him to call me."

"I will, Pastor, I will."

*   *   *

That week Paul had a lot of other things on his mind, but he couldn't stop thinking about Reiner. He hoped to hear something soon, and he couldn't imagine what his next step should be if Reiner didn't call. Paul struggled with sermon scribbling on Thursday, but wasn't satisfied with what he had written. On Friday morning he came to the office promising himself he would have the sermon done before noon.

"Pastor, call on line 2," Carol announced.

"Good morning, this is Pastor Paul."

"Good morning, Pastor, this is Maria Olivera."

"Hello, Maria, how are you this fine morning?"

"I am fine, Pastor; but I have a problem."

"Perhaps I can help you with it. You want to tell me about it?"

"I'm kinda worried about a phone call I had las' night about nine o'clock."

"That is rather late. Who was it?"

"I'm not sure, he didn't say, but I think it was that Mr. Holtz who joined Trinity las' fall."

Oh, oh, not again! Paul's heart rate jumped up. "You recognized his German accent?"

"Si. And I tell you what he say to me, he say, 'No way in hell we're letting you Mexicans take over our country!"

Paul winced and took a deep breath. *This has got to stop!* he thought to himself.

"He say some other very nasty things, and I was scared, so I hung up."

"That was the right thing to do, Maria." Paul wasn't sure what to say next. "I'll have a talk with Reiner, with Mr. Holtz, and tell him he can't be making phone calls like this."

"I don't know what to do, Pastor, so I call you. I hope you can do somet'ing."

"I'll do what I can, and get back to you, Maria. I don't think Reiner would actually do anything to harm you. I'm sorry Reiner spoke to you this way."

"Thank you, Pastor, thank you."

Paul hung up, thought for a moment, and picked up the phone again, and dialed.

"Hello, Tillie, this is Pastor Walker, have you heard from Reiner? Has he come home yet?"

"No, Pastor, I haven't heard from him at all. I'm getting very worried."

"Have you thought of where he might have gone?" Paul asked.

"He has a brother in New York, but they don't get along. I don't think he went there."

"Why don't you give him a call and ask if he's heard from Reiner."

"Okay, Pastor, I'll do that. Goodbye."

Paul hung up, thought for a moment, looked up a number in his roll-a-dex, picked up the phone and dialed again.

"Weston Police, Sergeant Mayfield, how may I help you?"

"Hello Sergeant, this is Pastor Paul Walker, I'm trying to reach Detective Sean Asplund." Paul had worked with Detective Asplund who had investigated Brian Holloway's homicide.

"He's not in the office right now, but I can have the dispatcher give him a message."

"Would you please have him call me at Trinity Lutheran Church? Thank you."

"I'll get the message to him right away."

A few minutes later, Sean returned the call. Paul explained his problem to the detective. "It's good to hear from you again, Pastor. I'll do some checking on Reiner Holtz and see if I can find him for you."

The next few days were anxious ones for Paul, and for Tillie, Miguel, Maria, and Cheri. Fortunately, Reiner had not contacted the Arriaga family. Paul debated whether or not to call and warn them about Reiner. Rather than upset them unnecessarily, he decided to wait and hope Reiner did not know how to reach them. Sean Asplund called at Paul's office on Monday morning. "Good news, Pastor, I've located Reiner Holtz. He's registered at the Best Western Motel at the south end of town."

"I really need to talk with him, Sean, but I don't know what to expect."

"Then I strongly suggest you not go alone. Would you like me to accompany you?"

"I was hoping you'd say that!" Paul laughed.

"Sure, no problem. Let me take care of a couple things and I'll pick you up at the church this afternoon. Is one o'clock okay?"

"Yeah, that would be great. I really appreciate this, Sean. See you then."

That afternoon, Sean and Paul climbed the stairs to Room 232 at the Best Western. The sky was overcast, and the air seemed unusually warm. Paul usually loved spring, but today just seemed gloomy. Paul was reminded of his first visit at Reiner's home, the full moon and clouds, the eerie warm air. Paul knocked on the door.

A voice spoke from inside. "Yah, who is it?"

"Pastor Paul Walker, Reiner. I'd like to talk with you."

"Go avay! I don't vant to talk."

"Tillie's been real worried about you, Reiner. I won't take but a minute. May I come in?"

"Nah. Tell Tillie I'm okay . . . . Not to worry. I DON'T VANT TO TALK."

Sean whispered in Paul's ear, "Do you want me to tell him it's the police?"

"No, not yet," Paul whispered back. He thought for a minute about the conspiracy theory which seemed to have Reiner so upset. "Reiner, I've been thinking about what you said." Paul paused. "I think you may be right about the Mexicans. I hadn't realized how powerful they've become. I didn't know about all the wars going on among the drug lords." Paul stopped and listened. It sounded like movement inside.

Reiner looked out the peek hole in the door. "Who's that with you?"

"I brought my friend, Sean Asplund. He's a detective and he's investigating . . . uh . . ." Paul was thinking rapidly, "investigating illegal aliens. We both thought you might be able to help us."

Reiner began to wonder if perhaps the pastor was beginning to understand. His defenses weakened. He unbolted the door and opened it slowly. "Willkommen," he said reluctantly, using the German word for *welcome*. Reiner looked awful. He hadn't shaved for a week. His eyes were bleary. A smoky haze filled the room. The laptop sat open on the bed next to a yellow legal pad full of scribbling. The phone book and church directory also lay on the bed. Reiner pointed to two chairs next to the table by the window. Paul pulled the dark curtains back slightly. He and Sean took the chairs, and Reiner sat on the bed and pushed his laptop aside. The room smelled of rotting food, filthy clothing, tobacco, and perspiration.

"It's getting late, Pastor." Reiner stared, first at Paul, then at Sean. His breath smelled awful.

"It's about two in the afternoon, Reiner." Paul wasn't sure what Reiner meant by "late."

"I'm not talking about the time of day." Reiner's eyes were shifting rapidly now. His voice sounded parched. "I'm talking about the problem in Mexico."

"Yes, the drug cartels are causing a lot of trouble." Paul thought if he played along he might draw Reiner into a discussion. The more Reiner talked, the more Paul would be able to diagnose what was happening and what his mental state might be.

"Ha!" Reiner yelled. "Zat's a red herring!"

"I don't understand," Sean interjected. "What do you mean by that?"

"While everyone is concerned about drug wars south of the border, no one is paying attention to the real problem."

"Which is?" Paul asked.

"The Mexican plot to reclaim the United States!" Reiner looked at them with incredulity.

"Tell me more about this plot, Reiner." Paul didn't want to shut him down.

"The evidence is here, on the internet," Reiner slurred, pointing at his laptop. His eyes flashed rapidly between Paul and Sean, the laptop and the door. "The Mexican government is sending troops to the border. They say they are fighting the drug lords, but they are really preparing an invasion! It's a brilliant plan. The Mexicans who are already in this country are preparing too. They're serving as informants, letting their government know where our army bases are, and how many troops and tanks we have near the border. Did you know that all of Texas and New Mexico, Arizona and California, used to be part of Mexico? The damn Mexicans want it back! And in a matter of weeks, maybe days now, they'll have it!"

Reiner was ranting, unable to turn off his obsessive vision. "I've seen it coming for months . . . ze handwriting on ze wall. The signs have been there all along. All we have to do is connect the dots. It's getting late. Time's up. Don't say I didn't warn you." His hands began fumbling with the laptop. He began mumbling incoherently. "They're coming. I tell you, zey are going to take over."

Paul looked at Sean. Sean looked at Paul. They tried to communicate as much as possible without speaking. Sean reached down and touched his handcuffs, then looked up. His eyes questioned Paul, *"Do you want me to use them?"* Paul thought for a moment, then, shook his head no.

"Reiner," Paul continued, "we need your help. If the Mexicans are going to be stopped, we need to notify the governor, the president, call out the National Guard."

"I've sent emails to all ze authorities, and so far zer has been no response."

"Reiner, they're not going to listen to you. But if they get a call from the Weston Police and if a Lutheran pastor verifies the warning, then they'll listen. Come with us, Reiner. We need your help." It was a stupid plea, but Reiner was so agitated, Paul hoped he would buy it.

Reiner looked from Paul to Sean who was rising from his chair. "We need you at headquarters," Sean added, gesturing for Reiner to follow them to the door. Sean wasn't sure what they would do once they got Reiner into the patrol car, but he thought Paul must have a plan. Paul also stood up and put his hand out to Reiner. Reiner grasped Paul's hand and rose from the bed. Paul looked him in the eye, trying to confirm a pact. "We're in this together," Paul added.

They made their way down the hall, down the stairs, past the lobby, and out to the car. Paul made several comments to reassure Reiner how much they needed him. As he guided Reiner into the back seat and closed the door, he moved around the car next to Sean who was standing by the driver's door. "Let's head for the hospital psych unit," he whispered.

Sean grinned, "I'm glad you didn't say let's take him to police headquarters." Paul smiled back and climbed into the back seat next to Reiner. Paul stared seriously at Reiner and said, "Good. You're doing the right thing, Reiner."

Sean drove toward the hospital in Gary hoping Reiner wouldn't ask any questions.

Paul began praying, *Dear God, we need your help. Reiner needs help, but I don't want to do this against his will. How can I get him to cooperate and enter the hospital voluntarily? Lord, I need your help.*

"Reiner," Paul began tentatively, "I hope you know how much I and all the members at Trinity are pleased you joined our church."

"Yah, Pastor, I know."

"I hope you realize that I really do want to help you."

Reiner didn't answer. He sat staring ahead at the traffic.

"Reiner, it seems to me that you haven't been your 'old self' lately." Still no reply from Reiner.

"I sure wish I could see that 'happy Reiner' again," Paul continued.

Reiner continued staring straight ahead, then spoke with no emotion, "Happy is for children."

Sean continued driving. Paul prayed again, *Please God, guide this conversation. Let your Holy Spirit give me the right words to say.* "Oh Reiner, don't you remember when you and Tillie first were married? You were happy then, weren't you?"

"Yah, I vas happy. Tillie vas a lovely bride. She is still a wonderful woman. But we were children . . . foolish children in love."

"Do you ever feel filled with joy?" Paul asked.

"Joy? We won't know joy until we are in heaven."

"What about contentment? Do you ever feel deeply content, Reiner?"

"Only those who are naïve are content, Pastor."

"Oh Reiner, I'm really worried about you."

"Yah, me too. Sometimes I zink I'm losing it."

"Losing what?"

"Everyzing! I used to feel like I had control, but not anymore."

"You're losing control?" Paul glanced at Reiner as the squad car crossed into Gary, only a few more miles to the hospital. Sean was nervous about what might happen when they got to their destination and so was Paul.

"Yah, I don't know vas is los," Reiner said, using an old German expression.

"Maybe our good and gracious God is trying to tell you to 'let go and let God,' Reiner."

"Let God what?"

"Let God have control. Trust God. Faith means placing our trust in God."

"I have faith, Pastor. I believe in God. I believe God will take care of everyzing after I die. But while I'm living, I must be in control! I believe zat is what God wants of me."

"Reiner, maybe God wants you to come to him like a little child," Paul glanced again and decided to repeat those words, "like a little child . . . carefree and trusting . . . happy and joyful. Was there ever a time in your childhood when you felt happy and joyful?"

Reiner did not reply. Paul looked at him again and remembered Reiner's stories about his childhood in Nazi Germany. "I think God sent me to you today, Reiner, so you could be a child again; but this time He wants you to be a happy child. Maybe God has sent me to take care of you. I hope you'll trust me, Reiner." A tear ran down Reiner's cheek.

Sean turned into the hospital driveway and pulled up to the emergency entrance. Reiner looked at the hospital and asked, "Where are we? Zis is not the police station. Zis is ze hospital."

"I need to talk to a friend," Paul replied as he climbed out of the back seat. "I'll only be a minute. Sean, would you wait here with Reiner?"

"Sure thing." Sean started fiddling with the police radio hoping to distract Reiner.

Reiner was confused. *Why were they at a hospital?* He was anxious to get to the police station. "Why can't we just call headquarters from your squad car, detective?" Reiner asked.

"Reiner, this is just too critical a matter to be handled over the radio. I'm sure you understand."

Reiner seemed to agree, and moved back slightly in his seat. He leaned his head back and let out a deep sigh. In a few minutes Paul reappeared with several orderlies following him out the emergency room doors. Paul opened the back door of the car and asked Reiner to please get out. Reiner pulled back and asked again, "What's going on?" One of the orderlies moved around to the other door.

"Reiner, I want to help you. These men are here to help you too. Please come with them." Paul reached in for Reiner's hand. Reiner looked at the number of men surrounding him and slowly climbed out of the car. He became more clearly aware of the reality around him. They were at a hospital. They weren't going to the police station. "Please trust me," Paul begged. "Let God take over, Reiner. It's too much for us. It's time to let go. Let God take care of you for awhile."

Reiner thought that might be what he needed. He walked slowly toward the emergency room doors flanked by Paul and three orderlies. *I'm going into the hospital,* Reiner thought to himself. *I've never been so confused. Maybe they'll help me get better.*

Sean had his handcuffs ready. One of the orderlies held a straight jacket behind his back. Paul and Sean were both relieved that Reiner didn't put up a fight. They walked into the ER and Reiner sat peacefully in a wheel chair while Paul gave as much admitting information as he could. One of the doctors came out of the unit to talk to them and asked Reiner to sign the admitting papers and consent for treatment. Reiner nodded and signed. Paul sat down next to him and did his best to reassure him. "You'll be here a couple of days, Reiner, while they do an evaluation. I promise you I'll stay in touch. I'm also going to notify Tillie so she won't worry about you. Okay?"

After almost an hour, Paul and Sean walked back out the emergency room doors into the sunny fall day. "Phew! That went better than I expected," Paul confessed.

"I can't believe we didn't need to use the cuffs," Sean replied. "That was a lot of fast talking you did at the motel."

"I can't believe it either," Paul agreed. "I think we both just witnessed a small miracle."

"Maybe a big miracle!" Sean added.

Emotionally exhausted, they slumped into the patrol car. Paul asked, "Do you mind if I say a prayer?"

"Not at all," Sean replied. "In fact, I'd appreciate it."

"Dear Lord, forgive me for being just a little deceitful to Reiner. You know I meant it for his own good. I think, when we got to the hospital, he realized he needs a different kind of help. I pray the coming days will go well for him and for Tillie, and that, perhaps with some rest and medication and counseling, he'll be able to return home without his obsession and conspiracy theories. Oh, and Lord, thanks for Sean. I really appreciate his being with me today. God bless him and all peace officers who protect and serve. Amen."

"Thanks, Pastor." Sean turned the key in the ignition and drove Paul back to Trinity. Back in his office, Pastor Paul called Tillie and asked if he could stop by for a visit. He explained what had happened at the motel and reassured her that Reiner was in good care. They arranged to go to the Best Western the next day to pick up Reiner's laptop and clothing. Paul also offered to drive her to the hospital to see Reiner.

Tillie was thankful that the pastor offered to drive her to the motel on Tuesday. The desk clerk asked for both their ID's before giving them the room key. He also wanted Tillie to pay for the room rent due. Reiner had paid for his first week, but owed for the past two days. He wouldn't take a check, but accepted her VISA card. When they opened the room and stepped inside, Tillie looked at the mess, shook her head, and sighed, "Oh, Reiner." She gathered up the dirty clothes which were strewn around the room and stuffed them into Reiner's suitcase. Paul picked up the laptop and church directory, and they returned to the car. As they climbed into the front seat, Paul asked Tillie, "Are you ready to go to the hospital today and visit Reiner?"

"Yes, Pastor, I'd appreciate that very much. I do hope he's going to be all right."

"I hope so, Tillie. I hope so too."

16

Scratch paper can be found in most offices. Some people call it scrap paper, though it is still usable, if at least one side is blank. In England it's called a "scribbling pad." Paul had a stack of scratch paper in his desk which Carol, his secretary, was kind enough to keep renewing with mistakes from the office copy machine. It was handy for writing shopping lists and reminders of "things to do." When the task was done and the reminder was no longer needed, it was easy to toss the note into the waste basket. Young people use their phone or iPad, but Paul still jotted reminders on his scratch paper.

Liz Sterling was enjoying her little prank. Once a week, but not every week . . . it all depended on opportunity . . . she would slip into the pastor's office and pick up a note or two from the corner of his desk. She was having fun deciding what to do with them. Sometimes she would push them onto the floor. Occasionally she would drop one into the wastebasket. And sometimes she put them in her purse and took them to her realty office and disposed of them there. If asked, she would say it was just harmless fun; but to Paul, who kept losing notes, it was becoming a disturbing mystery. It was becoming annoying and frustrating. And THAT is the real reason Liz kept doing it.

Liz was also looking for patterns, habits, anything she might be able to use against Paul some day. Don't they say: *Information is power?* The note which had been the most helpful so far was the one which said simply: *Call Global Travel.* That one turned out to be a gold mine.

On this particular morning, the pastor was visiting someone at the hospital who was having surgery. Carol said he might not be back for an hour. Liz sat down at the table in the office with the checkbook and bills that needed to be paid. She put her purse on the floor next to her chair and proceeded to sign checks. Carol had just opened a box of Sunday School materials and wanted to take them to the Sunday School supply room, so she asked Liz to answer the phone if it rang. Liz assured her she would.

As soon as Carol was out of sight, Liz ducked into the pastor's study and picked up a note from the corner of his desk. She hurried quickly back to her seat and the checkbook, but took a quick glance at the note: *Call Tillie re: visit with Reiner.* She reached down to tuck it into her purse just as the pastor came through the door. Looking up from her purse, she said quickly, "Good morning, Pastor."

"Oh, good morning, Liz," Paul replied, only slightly startled to see her there in the office.

"I heard one of our members was having surgery this morning. How did it go?" Liz asked.

"They're running behind on the surgery schedule, so it won't be until eleven o'clock. I said a prayer, and the family said I didn't have to stay." At that moment Carol came back into the office and was startled to see the pastor back already.

"Oh, Pastor! I didn't expect you back for an hour or two."

"I was just explaining to Liz that the surgery won't start until eleven because they had an emergency surgery. Bob's surgery got bumped 'til later." Paul moved toward the door of his study. "Guess I'll just go back this afternoon and see how he's doing."

Paul sat down at his desk, said a silent prayer for Bob, and tried to remember what else was on his agenda for today. He glanced at the corner of his desk for the note he had put there before going to the hospital. It wasn't there. He was sure he had written a reminder. What was it? Oh yeah, *Call Tillie.* He thought, if he had time, he would take Tillie to the hospital this afternoon to visit Reiner who had been under psychiatric care for almost a month. Paul frowned, *another missing note.*

Paul got up from the desk and walked to the door. "Carol, have you seen the note I wrote this morning about calling Tillie Holtz?" Carol turned to face the pastor, and behind her, at the table, Liz glanced down at her purse on the floor.

"No, I haven't," Carol answered.

Paul's eyes went to the purse. There, next to the purse on the floor, was a piece of scratch paper, like the one he had written on. "May I see that scratch paper, Liz?" Paul asked, pointing toward the purse.

Liz looked down, horrified. The note she had taken from Paul's desk had not slipped into her purse but beside it, landing on the floor. She quickly reached down, grabbed it, and tucked it into the purse. "Oh, that's just a note about one of the bills I need to watch for," she said to Paul.

"May I see it?" Paul asked again.

"It's personal," Liz said, flustered. "It's for one of our expenses at home. Phillip said he'd pay it, so I wrote the note to remind him."

Paul stared at Liz, not believing a word. Liz looked down at the checkbook and started writing. Carol looked from one to the other, not sure what was going on, though she could feel the tension between them. Paul looked at Carol, then back at Liz who would not look up. He was tempted to walk over and remove the note from her purse. Instead, he turned and went back into his office to calm down . . . and call Tillie.

Liz closed up the checkbook and placed it back in the file drawer. She smiled and said good-by to Carol, picked up her purse and left the office. As she got into her car her face was set in bitter determination. *Paul Walker . . . what a mistake . . . why did we ever call him to Trinity? So help me, you'll learn you can't embarrass Liz Sterling and get away with it.*

17

Liz had been waiting for almost six months. The check for $6,845.87 to pay for their trip to Australia had cleared the bank without question. It had drawn down the Pastor's Discretionary Fund to under $200. In the months that followed, Liz continued transferring odd amounts from $85 to $149 from the general fund into the Pastor's Fund. One month she used the Fund to pay her own electric bill, making the check payable to Northern Indiana Power. She was careful not to put her own account number on the check, but simply placed it in the envelope with the invoice.

Liz was ready to spring the trap. September seemed like the ideal month; she would plead lack of focus and attention to details during the summer. She thought about how she would act through the whole ordeal, uncertain what to do, afraid of hurting the pastor's reputation, as naïve as possible. Howard Bardwell had been elected president of the congregation council last February, so he was still fairly new in the position. She might have to give him suggestions if he seemed unwilling to act. She called from home after dinner. "Hello, Howard, this is Liz Sterling."

"Hi, Liz, how are you this evening?"

"Pretty good . . . actually, a little confused and not sure what to do. That's why I'm calling."

"What can I help you with?" Howard asked, expressing concern.

"I found something rather strange when I was preparing the treasurer's report for the September council meeting. At first I thought I was just letting my imagination run wild, so I didn't say anything at the meeting. But that was a week ago, and it's still bothering me. That's why I decided to call you. Something's wrong. Maybe you can help me figure it out."

"I'm not the best bookkeeper in the world, but I'll help if I can."

"Can we meet at the church tomorrow? I know it's Saturday, but you have a key don't you?" Liz wanted to be certain the pastor was not around.

"Yes I do. What time would you like to meet?"

"Does ten o'clock work for you?" she asked.

"I'll see you at ten. Now don't you fret;" Howard reassured her, "we'll get this straightened out."

"Thanks, Howard. I'll feel so relieved just to talk it over with someone."

The next morning Liz gathered her reports and a recent print out of the on-line report showing details of transactions from the Discretionary Fund.

Howard unlocked the door and they went upstairs to the meeting room near the office. "Well, Liz, what seems to be the problem?" Howard asked when they were seated.

"It's the Pastor's Discretionary Fund," Liz answered. Howard waited while she pulled reports from her bag. "I haven't paid much attention to things this summer. You know, I've paid the bills; but other than that I haven't been focused on my treasurer's duties."

"We all tend to relax in the summer and let things slide," Howard replied sympathetically. "Did you say Pastor's Discretionary Fund? I didn't know he had one."

"I didn't either, until I became treasurer," Liz replied. "I guess the pastor wanted it kept kinda private."

"Mm-hmm," Howard nodded and waited for Liz to continue.

"He used to tell me how thankful he was to be able to help members and people in the community, and keep the gifts anonymous. Shortly after I became treasurer he explained how he used the fund to provide cash gifts to help people with their rent or utility bill or to buy groceries. He asked me simply to transfer a small amount, say $100 to $200 each month from the general fund into the Discretionary Fund . . . just whatever you feel can be spared, he said."

"Hmmm," Howard was nodding his head in affirmation, but a troubled frown had appeared.

Before sliding the report in front of him, Liz asked casually, "Do you remember what month it was that Pastor and Cheri took that trip to the Holy Land?"

"I think it was back in February, right after the meeting when I was elected president," Howard answered.

That's what I was thinking. Normally, I wouldn't question what the pastor was doing. Helping others is what the church *should* be doing. But look at this . . ." Liz pointed at the bank report showing the check, paid to Global Travel, January 28th, in the amount of $6,845.87.

"Dear Lord!" Howard gasped. His eyes met Liz's.

"My reaction exactly," Liz replied. "What should we do?"

Howard thought for a minute.

"At first I thought I should ask the pastor about it," Liz continued. "But then I got really nervous and thought he might make up some lame story. Then I thought maybe I shouldn't warn him and give him time to cover his mistakes. I just didn't know what to do!" Liz was sounding very panicky.

"I'm glad you called me," Howard said, trying to reassure Liz that she had done the right thing. "I suppose we need to look into this further, and make sure we're not imagining something that isn't true."

"That's kind of what I was thinking too" Liz agreed. "Maybe we should turn this over to the police and let them investigate it. I'm sure they have more expertise than we do." Liz was pleased with how this was going. *What could be worse for a pastor than being arrested for suspicion of fraud? How would he explain THAT to his wife and congregation?*

"I suppose you're right," Howard replied hesitatingly. "I hate to get the police involved; but maybe that's the best thing to do at this point."

"We're not really accusing him of anything," Liz added, wanting to reassure the president he was doing the right thing.

"That's true. But I've got another idea. Why don't we just get an independent auditor to do an audit of the accounts?

Liz was not too keen on this idea. She envisioned a public scandal with Paul being dragged off in handcuffs. "I suppose they could tell us if funds are missing, but could they tell us who did it?"

"I don't know. But I do think an audit is a good idea," Howard replied. "I'd rather not have the police involved until we know more about what happened."

"You're probably right," Liz agreed reluctantly.

"I'll call our attorney, Miguel Juarez; I'll bet he could suggest a good accountant."

"Good idea!" Liz smiled and nodded in affirmation, but felt a twinge of discomfort as she saw the whole thing moving out of her control.

"Based on what you've shown me already, I'm sure the council would agree that an audit is an excellent idea, even if the church does have to pay for it. Heck, I'd be willing to pay for it myself just to get this cleared up."

Howard Bardwell was confident this was the best possible next step, and it needed to be done.

"I'll be glad to turn over any records and tell them whatever I can. I just don't know that much about it," Liz said innocently. "Oh, I hope the pastor's not going to get in trouble over this."

"Me too," Howard agreed, nodding his head and wondering how this would all turn out.

18

Paul had no idea what was happening behind the scenes. October was an exciting month for the Walkers. Their son Chip was in his senior year at Weston High. Randy, a junior, was playing on the varsity basketball team this fall. On this particular Friday night Randy was nicely dressed and sitting in front of the television watching a sitcom. Paul joined him on the sofa. A few minutes later, Cheri appeared in brown slacks and a bright yellow sweater. "Wow, Mom! You look great!" Randy had a way of lifting people's spirits with his flattering, but sincere compliments. Paul smiled, feeling very proud of both his son and his wife.

"Chip, we're ready to go!" Paul hollered down the hall.

"Be there in a minute, Dad," Chip yelled back. It seemed Chip was always running late.

Tonight was the first performance of his senior year for the symphonic band. Throughout his junior year, Chip had enjoyed his deepening friendships with members of both the marching band and symphonic band. Paul and Cheri were proud of his dedication to the trumpet. He held the position of first chair for most of the year. They were also proud of his scholastic achievements in math and science. Chip was accepted at Indiana University and planned to major in computer science. Paul wasn't sure where that interest had come from; neither he nor Cheri was that fond of computers. It just seemed to be the exciting new field for students who had grown up with video games. Paul thought it was really funny when he first called his son, our "Computer Chip." But for some reason, Chip just gave his dad a dirty look.

As Randy, Paul, and Cheri moved into the garage, Chip appeared in his black slacks and white long-sleeved shirt, trumpet case in hand. They climbed into the car as the garage door was opening. "Look, Mom, I remembered!" Chip held up his trumpet. Cheri laughed, remembering the frantic drive to the homecoming parade during his sophomore year.

"But we are running a little late, Chip," his dad taunted him. "Some things never change."

At the school concert hall, families were milling about, greeting friends and finding seats. Paul and Cheri spoke to several couples while Randy chatted with his friends. The lights dimmed momentarily, indicating that people should take their seats. A few minutes later, the hall was darkened and the curtains parted on stage. Mr. Hanson walked out from stage-right and bowed to the applause of the audience. The concert began with Aaron Copland's "A Lincoln Portrait," including a reading of Lincoln's words by the student council president. That was followed by several songs from "Porgy and Bess." The finale was a stirring composition, "The Wild Bears" by Edward Elgar.

The concert was magnificent! All the parents were amazed at the level of sophistication demonstrated by the band students. "I've got to remember to write a note of appreciation to Mr. Hanson," Paul commented to Cheri. "He's done wonders with these students!"

The evening was a mixture of excitement and pride for the band. Chip told his family he'd get a ride home with Jennifer. Several band members wanted to go to the local drive-in for hamburgers afterwards.

Chip's senior year was off to a good start, and so was Randy's junior year. Moving from JV to Varsity was the step he had dreamed about all the previous year. Through the month of September, he practiced with the varsity squad. He sat impatiently on the bench for most of the first three games. Finally, in late October, he got the call to start the game on the floor.

*   *   *

"Walker, I'm starting you at point guard tonight. Scott's got the flu." That's what Coach said to me at practice this afternoon. I'm only a junior, but honest to God, I think I'm better than Scott. Scott's a senior; I guess that's why Coach lets him play more than me. I could hardly wait to get home to tell Dad. My dad played basketball when he was in high school, but the game was a lot different back then. Next year, when I'm a senior, I should be starting every game!

I've played limited minutes in previous games this season, but tonight I'm gonna show Coach that I'm ready to lead the team and make the plays. Coach told us we would have to be tough-minded because our opponents, the Gary High Indians, are ranked number one in the league, and have a reputation for hard, physical play. I'm a little nervous because some of the players are a lot bigger than me. I'm quick. I'm a good passer. My shooting percentage is good. But I hate a lot of physical contact.

My whole family was at the game tonight. It had finally come, my first game in the starting line-up for the Weston Warriors. Man, I couldn't believe the crowd! Weston was as high on sheer enthusiasm as we could be! I was pumped! I waited for the announcer to call my name. "Starting tonight at point guard, number 1, RANDY WALKER!" I ran onto the court, and I swear I could hear my parents yelling louder than anyone. Our family, like most Hoosier families, goes crazy over basketball in the fall. Honest to God, the entire state of Indiana does nothing but eats, sleeps, and breathes b-ball. The noise in the gymnasium was deafening.

The Gary Indians won the opening tip and scored an easy lay-up. Stupid mistake on our part; one of our guys missed his assignment. I brought the ball down court, got double-teamed in the corner, and lost the ball, my first turn-over. Shit! Coach knew we all had a case of nerves, so he let us play and kept yelling encouragement. The Indians scored again. I brought the ball into the forecourt and made a quick bounce pass to our center who pivoted under the basket and scored for the Warriors! Our home crowd went crazy! It was good to have those first points on the board.

117

The Gary Indians got into a rhythm with hard, bumping, physical play at both ends of the court. I kept waiting for the referees to call a foul, but it was like they forgot their whistle. "Get physical!" Coach yelled from the sidelines. Next time down the court, I hooked my defender with my elbow as I turned the corner with the ball and drove to the basket. TWEEEET! Shit! I was called for the offensive foul! I couldn't believe it! "That's okay; that's okay!" Coach yelled and clapped his hands.

When the scoreboard read 12-2 in favor of the Indians, Coach called a time out to settle the team and give us a breather. "You guys are all jitters out there," he said. "Take some deep breaths and calm down. I want you to play hard. You've got to match their physical intensity . . . rough but not dirty . . . understand?" We all nodded. "Randy, I want you to stick on your man like glue. Don't give him an inch of space. You hear me? Stay in front of him; crowd him; annoy him; disrupt his passing and don't worry about his shooting. Got that?" I nodded yes.

When the horn blew to resume play, I was more determined than ever to play tough. I crowded my man on defense like Coach said, and I relaxed on offense with crisp passes and confident shots when I was open. And I was making shots! Slowly, the scoring gap was closing. Weston was only two points down when the buzzer sounded at the half.

In the locker room Coach told us we were playing well. "The Indians are a tough team, and we're in this game! Two points is nothing. We can win. The most important thing is not to let them beat us mentally. They love to intimidate. They wear teams down. But we're tougher! Right?" Coach repeated, looking for an answer, "We're tougher . . . RIGHT?"

"RIGHT!" we yelled.

The second half began just like the first. Gary out-muscled and out-hustled us at both ends of the court. The Indians again built the lead to eight points. Our coach called time out. I can't believe what he did next. He put a big, burly guard in for me and told me to sit on the bench. I was upset. When play resumed Coach came over to me and said, "Son, I want you to sit and watch for a few minutes. Watch how the Indians are moving the ball. Watch your teammates and get a feel for who's hot and who's not.

Concentrate on the game, not on your hurt feelings. I'll put you back in when the fourth quarter begins."

I looked up in the stands and saw my parents. I could tell by the look on their faces they were frustrated. They thought I was playing well, and they couldn't understand why the coach had benched me. The third quarter seemed to last forever, and when the horn blew, the Indians were up by twelve!

At the beginning of the fourth quarter, I couldn't wait to get back on the court. I was fresh and my defender was tired. Adrenalin was pumping and I felt like flying! My teammates caught fire and no one missed on our next seven attempts! In a matter of minutes, I scored four baskets and two free throws. When Weston tied the game, Gary's coach called time out.

Our bench was jumping up and down, and the fans were screaming! With two and a half minutes left in the game, I scored again, putting Weston up by two. This was my dream come true. Two minutes to play, Weston up by four! Momentum was all in Weston's favor. Gary's coach called another time out. Our coach encouraged us not to become over-confident. "Focus . . . concentrate . . . two more minutes. Play hard! Give your best effort and you'll win this one!"

Gary scored on their next possession. Weston scored on ours. Gary's point guard brought the ball up the court and drove hard from the left side of the court to the right. Their other guard set a screen and as I came by, he threw his elbow into my face. My head snapped back and I fell to the floor. The referee blew his whistle and came running over. Blood was flowing from my mouth. The next few minutes were a blur.

Weston's trainer ran onto the floor and the coach called time out. Paul and Cheri held their breath, wanting to run to their son, but waiting for fear of embarrassing him. Slowly, Randy sat up holding his mouth. The trainer and coach leaned over him a moment then lifted him to his feet. The crowd applauded as he walked slowly to the bench, blood dripping on the gym floor. He was handed a towel and the trainer walked him back to the locker room. At that point, Cheri and Paul came out of the stands and made their way to the locker room also. The worried look on their faces told many in the stands to move out of their way.

When they finally found Randy he was sitting on a bench holding a bloody towel and a tooth. The trainer had placed a wad of gauze in Randy's mouth and was telling him to hold an ice bag against his lip to reduce the swelling and pain. "You might want to get him into the dentist first thing tomorrow morning," the trainer suggested to his parents.

When I saw my parents in the locker room I realized I had been taken out of the game. I wanted to get back on the floor, so I said to the trainer, "Can I go now?"

"Yeah, take the ice bag with you . . . . But you're not playing!" the trainer shouted as our family left the locker room. As we walked down the hall we saw the crowd exiting the gymnasium, but it was too quiet. There were no shouts of victory. As we came through the doors into the gym, it was obvious that Weston had lost the game. The scoreboard read Home: 64—Visitors: 67. My head dropped. "I wish I could have finished the game," I said to my parents. "I think we would have won if I had stayed on the court."

"Tough loss, son, a really tough loss," Dad replied. He wrapped his arm around my shoulder.

My friend Jason came running over, "It was a dirty play! They hit you on purpose."

"Well, it's not right to accuse them of dirty play," my dad replied. "We don't know that it was intentional."

"Aw, c'mon Mr. Walker, you saw how he swung his elbow into Randy."

"Maybe you're right," my dad added, "but all I can say is I'm very proud of you, son." Dad stood in front of me and looked straight at me, "Randy, you played a darn good game!"

"Thanks, Dad, I thought I did too." My mouth hurt, but it felt good to have such a supportive family.

As we moved down the hall, Mom said, "I do think we should have the dentist look at that tomorrow. We'll have to get a bridge or glue that tooth back in, if that's possible."

In the parking lot a subdued crowd of students and parents made their way to their cars. Several of my friends came over to ask how I was. They said, "Good game." But I think they were just trying to encourage me.

*   *   *

A couple of weeks later I overheard my parents talking late one evening. "Can you believe the bills from the dentist and orthodontist?" Mom was saying.

"Fifteen hundred between the two!" Dad replied.

"How much did the insurance cover?" Mom asked.

"Almost a thousand, thank goodness. But that still leaves over five hundred out of our pocket."

I was nervous when I heard Mom say, "Maybe I should go back to work."

Then I was relieved when Dad said, "Not a chance! We love having you home! You spoil us all."

I was shocked when I learned how much that elbow in the mouth would cost my parents. But thank God, they're not arguing about it. Everyone at school has been asking about my injury and wanting to see my new tooth. Everybody says their player did it on purpose. I know that's just poor sportsmanship; and I agree with Coach and my parents . . . that's not winning, no matter what the scoreboard says!

It was nice to get so much attention, but losing the game hurt almost as much as losing the tooth. Next year, I swear, will be a win for Weston!

19

A Certified Public Accountant

offered to meet her at the church office, but Liz wanted to keep the pastor unaware of what was happening as long as possible. She made an appointment with the accountant at his office on Tuesday afternoon. Liz stopped at the church at noon and picked up the checkbook for the General Fund. She had gathered up the other files and reports from her office at home and placed them in the trunk of her car that morning. Only the checkbook for the Pastor's Discretionary Fund was left at home, intentionally. Her plan was to plant it in the pastor's office without him knowing it was there. Whoever was investigating would find it. Paul would be flustered, claiming he knew nothing about it.

The accountant explained to her that an audit would review the accounts, and present an opinion as to the accuracy of the financial condition of the organization; and if necessary, make recommendations on accounting practices within the organization. She and the accountant went through the list of Trinity's funds: General Fund, Building Maintenance Reserve Fund, Scholarship Fund, Memorial Fund, and Pastor's Discretionary Fund. She presented bank statements for the past nine months, back to, and including January. Liz pointed out that she didn't know where the checkbook was for the Discretionary Fund; she assumed the pastor had it. Then, she pointed to the bank statement of the Discretionary Fund, showing the large check written to Global Travel last January which had caused her concern.

"That would be an internal matter," the accountant explained. "If the fund is to be administered at the pastor's discretion, how he uses that fund is not the auditor's concern."

"But . . . but he can't use it to pay for his own vacation!" Liz replied indignantly.

"And that's why I said it is an internal matter within the organization," the auditor replied.

Liz sat there dumbfounded.

The accountant began questioning her about procedures. "Are two signatures required on all checks written? How often are funds audited? Who does the audit? Who has access to the funds? What about past treasurers?" Liz struggled to provide answers, embarrassed to realize how lax the church had been, still puzzled by the accountant's reaction, or non-reaction, to the pastor's obvious impropriety.

"Will you demand to see the checkbook for the Discretionary Fund?" Liz asked.

"We can only work with the information you give us. If you are not willing or able to turn over certain records voluntarily, the checkbook for instance, our audit will state that our opinion is based on the information given us."

"You mean . . . you can't get a search warrant or subpoena or something?" Liz was incredulous.

"No, ma'm. To proceed with a criminal investigation would be up to the Board of Directors of your organization."

"I see . . . I think I understand." Liz was upset. This wasn't going according to plan. She was hoping for a big surprise for the council and a dramatic arrest of the pastor. Maybe Howard would be forced to call the police if the auditor wouldn't do it.

"By the way, are you willing to sign a *release form* giving us permission to access bank records?" the accountant asked.

"Certainly, certainly," Liz replied.

"We'll review the accounts and provide a formal report. It may take a week to ten days, but we'll be in touch."

"Please let me know if there is anything more I can do to help," Liz insisted as she rose to leave.

"We'll let you know," the accountant replied.

20

The Council meeting on Monday night was being dreaded by Howard Bardwell. Liz Sterling, however, was feeling a mixture of excitement, anticipation, and nervous fear. If all went well, the pastor she had loathed for the past eight years would be forced to resign. If not, God only knew what might happen. She anticipated Pastor Paul's shock and his plea of innocence; and she was delighted to think his protests would make him appear all the more guilty. As president of the congregation council, Howard had received the report of the auditor, and realized it was rather nebulous, concerning what he and Liz considered embezzlement from the Discretionary Fund. He had shared the report with Liz, and they agreed it should be brought before the council. The fact that it had to be dealt with internally created doubts and fears for her. The pastor had close friends on the council. She had so wanted the police to make a dramatic arrest!

The treasurer's report had been moved to the final item on the agenda by the president. Liz was becoming more and more nervous as the meeting dragged on. Finally, it was time for her report. She presented the figures for the General Fund and referred briefly to other accounts. Then she paused and looked across the table at Howard. "After meeting with our council president a couple of weeks ago, a decision was made to conduct an audit of our funds," Liz continued. "Howard and I agreed it would be good to have the audit done by an outside firm because there seemed to a problem with one of the accounts. I think I'll let him take it from here." Liz looked nervously to Howard.

Howard Bardwell opened the folder containing the letter from the CPA who had done the audit.

"Let me just read what the official letter says:" Howard began.

> "We have reviewed the accompanying balance sheets of Trinity Lutheran Church which was incorporated as a non-profit corporation in the state of Indiana on September 15, 1912. This review includes statements of income and cash flows for the fiscal year July 1, 1993 to June 30, 1994, in accordance with Statements on Standards for Accounting and Review Services issued by the American Institute of Certified Public Accountants. All information included in these financial statements is the representation of the management of Trinity Lutheran Church.

> "A review consists principally of inquiries of church personnel and analytical procedures applied to financial data. It is substantially less in scope than an audit in accordance with generally accepted auditing standards. Based on our review, we are not aware of any material modifications that should be made to the accompanying financial statements in order for them to be in conformity with generally accepted accounting principles.

> "Policies regarding the use of designated funds are not within the purview of this report. Said policies are determined solely by your Board of Directors."

"In simple words," Howard continued, "our books are in order. The concern which Liz Sterling brought to my attention has to do with the Pastor's Discretionary Fund. Because the checkbook was not found, the CPA review simply states that "policies regarding the use of designated funds are determined solely by the Board of Directors," which in our case is the Congregation Council.

"Pastor's Discretionary Fund?" Pastor Paul Walker spoke up. "I didn't even know there was such a thing!" Several other council members voiced agreement, "Neither did I."

Darrel Thomas responded, "I've been around quite a while, and I think I do remember Pastor Bjornstad mentioning it once in a while."

"Well, I've never seen it or heard about it," Paul stated.

"Apparently, someone knows about it and has been using it," Howard began. "According to the bank statements, there have been regular deposits and occasional withdrawals from the account."

"Liz, do you know anything about this?" Paul turned his attention to the treasurer.

"Pastor, I'm really sorry, but I'm not sure what's going on. I think I need to tell the council about our discussion shortly after I became treasurer."

"What discussion was that?" Paul was extremely nervous. All his doubts and questions about Liz Sterling came to mind, and his stomach clenched into a knot.

"Well, surely you remember," Liz spoke calmly, knowing she had the upper hand. "I asked you about the Discretionary Fund, and you told me how you use it to help members who are in crisis, or even assist families in the community when you hear of a special need."

"I don't remember any such conversation," Paul replied, frowning and shaking his head. "Like I said, I didn't even know there *was* a Discretionary Fund."

"But Pastor, you said you wanted to help people anonymously, so they wouldn't be embarrassed about other members knowing of their financial problems. Don't you remember?"

"No, Liz, I don't remember any of that."

Liz pressed on, "You said I should transfer just a small amount each month from the General Fund, whatever I felt could be spared without depleting the needs of the budget."

Paul sat staring at her, stunned by her accusations, his anger building. She sounded so believable, but she was clearly lying. "That is simply not true," he said angrily.

The entire room was silent for what seemed like an eternity. Everyone was stunned to hear the pastor accuse the treasurer of lying. Howard Bardwell, as council president, was also quite uncomfortable. He realized it was up to him to move things along. He finally broke the silence, "Pastor, do you have the checkbook for the fund?"

"No, I do not," Paul said emphatically.

"Then how do you explain this?" Howard asked as he slid a photocopy of the checks which had been written on the account. "That is your signature on the checks, is it not?"

Paul grabbed the sheet and studied it, looking carefully at the signatures. "It looks like my signature. But I swear, I have never seen a checkbook, and I did not sign those checks."

"Are you saying, Pastor," asked Bonnie, "that someone forged your signature?"

"So it appears," answered Paul.

"Just for everyone's information," Howard continued, "there is one check, dated January 28, signed by the pastor, and made out to Global Travel, in the amount of $6,845.87."

"Isn't that when you and Cheri took that trip to the Holy Land?" Bonnie asked incredulously.

"Yes, but we paid for that trip ourselves. We used some money we inherited from Cheri's parents." Paul could hardly believe what was happening. It was pure crazy!

"Honestly, Pastor, I'd like to believe you, but this doesn't look good." Darrel really wanted to defend the pastor, but was shocked by the revelations.

"Same here," Jana chimed in. "I have so much respect for you, and have trusted you for so long. But these facts . . . I mean . . . that Global Travel check alone is shocking!"

Liz did her best to appear troubled, sorry to see the pastor in such a predicament. She noticed his hands resting nervously on top of his council notebook. There it was again. He was picking and tearing at one of his fingernails.

"I have an idea," interrupted Darrel, who desperately wanted to support his pastor and friend. "Pastor, you say you have never seen a checkbook for this account, and yet your signature appears to be on the checks. Would you mind if we went in your office and just looked around? Check in your desk drawers? I mean, just to be sure the checkbook is not in your possession?"

"He could have taken it home," Liz suggested, knowing full well where the checkbook was.

"No, I don't have the checkbook, here OR at home!" Paul replied emphatically. He could feel not only confusion and fear, but also his growing anger toward Liz Sterling.

It was just the reaction Liz had been waiting for. God bless Darrel for his wonderful suggestion. Liz had prepared the scene well. Knowing that the pastor would not be in the office on Friday afternoon, she had stopped at the church on Friday, about the time she thought the secretary would be leaving. Her timing was perfect. Carol was putting things away and getting ready to go when Liz walked in. "I'll be sure to lock the office when I leave," she promised Carol. As soon as Carol's car left the parking lot, Liz stepped into Pastor Paul's office. She opened the lower desk drawer and carefully tucked the Pastor's Discretionary Fund checkbook behind some file folders.

"Darrel, since it was your suggestion, I'd like to ask you and Bonnie to go into the Pastor's office and take a quick look through the drawers." Howard did not want to leave the meeting room, nor leave the pastor and treasurer in the room without his presence. As Darrel and Bonnie rose from their chairs, Howard continued, "Since the pastor didn't know any of this was coming, I don't think he would have taken the checkbook home or hidden it too well. Just take a look."

Once again, the room was silent. The sheet with copies of the checks from the Discretionary Fund was passed around the table, each council member examining it intensely. In a few minutes everyone looked up as Darrel and Bonnie returned to the room checkbook and ledger in hand. Paul's heart sank. "It was in the bottom drawer of the desk," Darrel announced sadly as he handed it to Howard.

"Someone must have put it there," Paul objected. Liz shook her head in disbelief. It was exactly the reaction she had been waiting for. It sounded so lame.

The president opened the ledger and glanced down the deposits and list of checks. "We'll need to examine this a little more closely, but it appears that the checks drawn on this account match the bank record." He paused and looked around the table. Paul's face was buried in his hands. "I'm sorry, Pastor," Howard said.

Fred Wilson, who had chaired the Call Committee nine years ago, had been quiet throughout the meeting, but finally spoke up. "This has been a difficult meeting for all of us. I think we need some time to reflect on what's happened here before any action is taken. If we act in haste we may regret it later on. Pastor Paul, I hope there is some explanation for all this. And if you have done something you regret . . . I hope you will offer your sincere apologies to all of us and to the congregation . . . and consider offering your resignation."

"I have nothing to apologize for, and no reason for resigning," Paul responded.

"I'd like to suggest we schedule a special council meeting a week from tonight," Howard spoke in conclusion. "Can everyone be here next Monday?" There were nods of consent around the table. "And I'd like to ask everyone here to maintain confidentiality. This is a most serious situation, and we don't need rumors flying through the congregation. Please, I urge you not to talk to anyone about this, not even your spouse." Howard looked around the table to let his words sink in. "One week, that's all I'm asking. I'm sure, after our meeting next Monday, we will get this resolved, one way or another."

Everyone looked around the table at the other members and at the pastor. Paul was staring at Liz. Liz, knowing she had lied, would not look at Paul.

Howard concluded, "This meeting is adjourned until next Monday at 7 pm. Let us pray. Lord of our lives and Lord of the church, we have been reminded again how easily things get out of control. We think we have our lives and institutions in order and under control, but we don't. Things can happen that we never anticipate. Once again we place ourselves in your hands. Hold us, sustain us, and guide us that we might do your will, and receive your blessing. These things we ask in Jesus' name. Amen."

Paul sat at the table as council members quietly left the conference room. He remembered his first meeting with Fred Wilson and the Call Committee, his interview, when he and Cheri were full of excitement, joy, and anticipation. He remembered all the Sundays mornings when members laughed and loved as they shared coffee and cookies. He thought of the potlucks, receptions for weddings, anniversaries, and funerals. Tonight, his church had become a courtroom and a hill called Calvary; and Paul felt like he had been crucified.

21

Paul couldn't sleep that night. He told Cheri the whole story when he got home from the meeting. He had been accused of misappropriation of church funds and of lying.

Cheri was in shock when she heard the details of what had happened. "But there's no way! No way!" she protested.

"I know. I know," Paul responded. "And I have this gut feeling that Liz Sterling is behind the whole thing. I just don't know how to prove it."

"Maybe you should call Miguel Juarez in the morning. He's always been willing to help us with legal matters," Cheri suggested.

"I suppose that would be a good thing to do, but I hope this can all be straightened out without going to court."

"What about your friend, Sean, on the police force?"

"No, no," Paul objected. "I hope we can resolve this without a criminal investigation. But I'll certainly keep Sean in mind."

Paul lay tossing and turning through the night. He kept reviewing the conversations at the council meeting and the most damning piece of evidence, the check to Global Travel. The amount did not match the cost of their trip . . . something didn't add up. At some point, around four or five o'clock, just as the sun was starting to light the sky, it figuratively "dawned" on him. He knew exactly what he needed to do the next morning.

As Paul rolled out of bed, Cheri opened her eyes and mumbled, "Good morning."

"Yes, it is," Paul answered. "It is a good morning. First, I'm going to call Miguel, as you suggested last night. If he agrees with my plan, I'm going to call Global Travel and clear up this whole mess." Paul dug through his records, pulling their itinerary for the trip to Israel, and the cancelled check from their personal checking account, proof that he had paid for the trip from their family funds. After breakfast Paul drove to the church and called Miguel. He explained exactly what had happened at the council meeting.

Miguel agreed that it looked bad for the pastor; then he asked several follow-up questions. "Do you have any idea who signed the check from your discretionary fund?"

"I have a hunch, but let me say again, it wasn't for our trip. We paid for our trip. It must have been for someone else's reservations." Paul went on to explain his intention to visit Global Travel to find out whose trip the check had paid for.

"I certainly hope you won't need legal representation, Paul, but if you do, you know where to reach me."

"Thanks, Miguel. I appreciate your support."

Paul dialed Global Travel and asked to speak to Julie who had made the reservations for their Holy Land trip. He made an appointment to see her at two-thirty. Next, he called Howard Bardwell and asked if they could meet at Global Travel Agency at two-thirty. Howard said he'd be there. Paul asked him to please bring the copy of the check he had supposedly written from the Discretionary Fund.

Paul walked out of his study, thanked Carol for starting the coffee, poured himself a cup, and returned to his office. His eyes focused on the corner of the desk where he always put his reminder notes. *An amazing coincidence,* he thought, *that not a single note has fallen in the wastebasket or disappeared in the past two months, since the day I confronted Liz.*

It was difficult to concentrate on anything except his anticipated meeting at Global Travel. He rehearsed the scene over and over again in his mind. He prayed he would return home this evening with proof that he was not guilty of embezzling funds.

At two-thirty he parked in the small gravel parking lot next to Globe Travel. As he opened the car door and climbed out, a cluster of fall leaves blew across his feet and under the car. *I know where I'd rather be right now,* Paul thought to himself, *on the golf course . . . enjoying fall colors and sinking a twelve foot putt.* He went in the front door of the travel agency and glanced around the office to see if Howard was already there. Julie was at her desk typing reservations for someone into her computer. Howard hadn't arrived yet.

Julie eyed Paul, smiled and held up a finger to indicate she'd be finished in a minute. Paul took a seat near the front door. A few moments later, Howard came in. He looked out of breath from rushing to get there, but Paul was relieved to see him. Julie rose from her desk and came to the waiting area. She looked neat and professional in heels, slacks, and fall sweater. Her long blond hair was pulled back in a pony tail and tied with a yellow scrunchie. Paul introduced her to Howard Bardwell and told him how much help she had been in planning the Holy Land trip. Julie smiled and returned the compliment, saying how much she had enjoyed working with Paul and Cheri. She invited them both to take chairs near her desk.

"Are you here to plan another trip, Pastor? Or is Mr. Bardwell planning to travel?" Julie asked.

"Actually, I've come to ask a favor, and I hope you can help me," Paul began in earnest.

"I'll do what I can, Pastor," Julie replied.

"Howard is the president of our congregation council, and I asked him to join me here because there are some issues about our reservations last February that need to be clarified." Julie listened and nodded. Paul continued, "Would you mind making a copy of our invoice? And, if you have it, a copy of the check I used to pay the account?"

"We don't make copies of the check, but the invoice should be marked paid in full. I remember when you wrote the check here in the office." Julie opened her computer records and opened the account for Paul Walker. She scrolled to the invoice and clicked "print" to make a copy. The printer hummed and out came the invoice for $4933.50, paid in full on January 18. She handed it to Paul who looked it over and handed it to Howard.

"Thanks, Julie, give us just a minute," Paul said. He opened the manila envelope he had brought from home and produced a copy of the same document. He also pulled out a copy of the cancelled check which was printed with his January bank statement. He showed both documents to Howard. Paul asked Howard, "Do you have a copy of that other check I made to Global Travel?"

"Yes, I've got it right here." Howard reached into his jacket pocket and removed a folded piece of paper which had been passed around the council meeting the night before. He handed it to Paul.

"Julie," Paul looked back to the travel agent, "Did you assist our church friends, Phillip and Elizabeth Sterling, with their travel plans in March this year?"

"Sterling . . . Sterling . . . hmm . . . I don't think so," Julie replied. "Maybe Debbie assisted them. Do you want me to ask her?"

"Yes, please," Paul answered. "They did an extensive trip to Australia and New Zealand in March."

Julie walked to Debbie's desk. Debbie was on the phone trying to book a plane flight. Julie stood there a moment, waiting. Debbie looked up. "I'm on hold. What do you need?"

"Just a quick question, did you help a couple by the name of Sterling book a trip to Australia and New Zealand last March?"

"Yes, I remember the Sterlings. What about them?"

"Nothing for now. Pastor Walker said he might have a question for you when you're through on the phone."

When Julie returned to her desk, Paul placed the document before her, showing the copy of a check for $6845.87 written to Global Travel and signed by him. She studied the page for a moment and then looked up at Paul with a puzzled expression. "This is dated January 27," she said. "Why would you write another check to Global Travel when you had already paid for your reservations?"

"Very good question," Paul answered. "One more favor. Would you look and see if this check paid for the Sterling's reservations?"

"I'm really sorry, Pastor, but I can't give out information about our clients."

"I'm not asking for anything I don't already know, Julie. I just want to make sure my second check paid their account in full."

"I'm not sure I should do this."

"You see my signature on the check for $6545.87. All you have to do is look back at their account and see if that matches the amount due on their invoice."

Somewhat reluctantly, Julie opened the Sterling's account. "Yes . . . that's all I can tell you. The amount due was paid in full by your check."

"And since I wrote the check, I would like a copy of that invoice," Paul insisted.

Julie hesitated. She wasn't supposed to give out information about other customers. But Paul's reasoning made sense. Finally she responded, "Since you paid it, I guess you have a right to a copy, to show it was paid in full."

"Thank you so much," Paul said, "I assure you that you're doing the right thing."

Julie hit "print" and handed the invoice to Paul who nodded and smiled a thank you. Paul examined the Sterling's invoice and handed it to Howard.

This time it was Howard who spoke with a sincere tone, "Thank you, Julie. We are most grateful for your help." He looked at the document. "Liz Sterling," was all Howard said to Paul.

"I suppose it's none of my business," Julie continued, "but it sure was nice of you to pay for the Sterling's trip to Australia."

"Yes . . . wasn't it," Paul replied with a sarcastic smile. As they rose to leave, Paul added, "Thanks, Julie. You don't know how much I appreciate this!" This time there was no sarcasm.

Julie smiled uneasily as she shook hands with both men. Something told her she didn't have the whole story.

*   *   *

On Sunday morning, several council members decided not to come to church. They didn't want to hear any gossip, and they didn't want to be part of spreading any. Paul's guilt seemed too obvious to deny, and they simply didn't want to face him. Paul himself was greatly relieved, knowing he would be exonerated on Monday. He wasn't sure he could have led worship otherwise.

The following Monday was an anxious one for Liz Sterling. She had set things up to look very bad for Paul, but since sharing her concern with Howard Bardwell, everything had escaped her control. Her prayer on Monday afternoon was that Pastor Walker would announce his resignation at tonight's meeting.

As council members gathered in the conference room a somber mood prevailed. When Pastor Paul came in, he was greeted politely but with reservation. Eyes kept probing, to see what kind of mood he was in, and attempting to assess what the next hour might hold. Howard Bardwell's entrance held no clue for them either. Liz sat quietly, nervously jiggling her foot.

Howard called the meeting to order, said a brief prayer, and reviewed the concerns raised at last week's meeting. "Since our last meeting, I have met with the pastor, and we have some additional information to share this evening." He glanced around the table at everyone's anxious faces. Liz looked away when his eyes met hers.

"The accusations made against our pastor are serious. He believes, as do we, that using church funds for personal benefit is a most egregious misappropriation."

Liz's foot continued jiggling wildly under the table.

"I have in my possession," Howard continued, "two documents which should clarify the confusion of last week. Pastor Walker is also in possession of copies, but we have not made others, because we don't feel it would be good for them to circulate in any way. I will explain these documents and anyone who wishes may examine them, but as I said, it is the only copy you will see.

"Last week, the pastor and I met at Global Travel to clarify the use of Discretionary Funds to pay for the Walkers' trip to the Holy Land. This first invoice, for Pastor Paul and Cheri's trip in February, is for $4,933.50 paid in full on January 18 from the Walker's personal funds. A check for that amount appears on the January statement from their bank." Howard paused to pass the copy of the Walkers' invoice around the table. At the same time, Paul passed a copy of the bank statement showing his personal check for $4,933.50. A bitter taste of bile moved into Liz's mouth.

"The second document is also from Global Travel, an invoice in the amount of $6,845.87, paid in full from the Pastor's Discretionary Fund, for a trip in March to Australia and New Zealand, taken by . . . Liz and Phillip Sterling."

Gasps could be heard around the table.

Bonnie was still trying to put the puzzle together. "But why would the pastor pay for the Sterlings' trip?" she asked.

"That's the point, Bonnie," Howard answered. "He didn't . . . . Liz Sterling wrote that check."

"I thought it had the pastor's signature on it," Bonnie insisted.

"We all thought so, last Monday night," Howard replied.

"I didn't write that check!" Liz objected. "I never saw that checkbook for the Discretionary Fund. It was in the pastor's desk; that's where Darrel found it!"

"Yes, Liz, that's where Darrel found it . . . after you put it there." Howard was leaning forward now and Liz was back-pedaling. It was all unraveling. Howard continued, "I took the liberty of looking at the checkbook for the General Fund which is kept locked in the file drawer in the office. Some of the notations were printed, not in script, in a hand printing which matched the printing in the Discretionary Fund ledger."

"NO!" screamed Liz. "I never had it! The pastor wrote those checks!"

"No, Liz, I'm afraid YOU wrote those checks . . . and forged the pastor's signature."

Liz began crying, sobbing hysterically. She grabbed her purse, ran out the door of the room, and left the church. A long silence followed her departure.

"Brothers and sisters in Christ, I'm afraid this meeting is far from over." Howard took a deep breath. "We have a long night ahead of us. We have some difficult decisions to make in regard to our treasurer. Our first order of business should probably be to appoint a new treasurer. Our second order of business is to decide whether or not to bring charges against Mrs. Sterling."

"Howard, may I make a suggestion?" Fred Wilson asked.

"Certainly."

"I think it would be wise to appoint a new treasurer tonight with an official motion from the council. That way, we could take care of the paperwork at the bank tomorrow. But I also think it would be wise, as we did last week, not to make any hasty decisions affecting Liz personally, until we've had time to think about this, and maybe talk to her about what happened."

Everyone nodded and voiced agreement. A new treasurer was appointed, and the meeting was adjourned with another strict reminder from Howard that everything be kept completely confidential. Another special meeting was called for the following Monday.

*   *   *

Howard received the letter of resignation from Liz on Thursday morning. Carol called to tell him a letter had arrived at the church office addressed to the Council President. The envelope and letterhead were from Weston Realty.

> *Dear Mr. Bardwell and members of the council:*
>
> *I am sorry that I will not be able to complete my term as treasurer of Trinity Lutheran Church. I am submitting my resignation immediately due to personal reasons. I wish you and the members of Trinity the very best.*
>
> *Sincerely, Liz Sterling*

He waited until Thursday evening to call Liz, not wanting to interrupt her at work. She answered the phone at home and sounded tired. Howard said he had received her letter and would share it with the council on Monday night.

"I'm very sorry about everything," Liz said, so softly Howard could barely hear her. "I guess I was just so resentful toward Pastor . . . I . . . I . . ."

"Liz, I accept your apology, and I have just one more question. I don't know if you've thought about it, but would you be willing to pay back the money you embezzled from the church?" Howard was quite certain the Sterlings were very capable, financially, of paying the debt.

There was a long silence. Howard waited. "Yes . . . yes, I suppose I should . . . Is the church going to bring charges against me?"

"I won't know until after our meeting on Monday," Howard replied. "but your willingness to repay the church might affect their decision. Would you like me to call you after the council meets?"

Again there was a long pause. "Yes, I guess so. Would you? I hope this doesn't get in the newspaper. My reputation could be ruined."

"I'll call next week. In the meantime, all I can suggest is that you keep praying."

*   *   *

At the meeting Monday night, Howard read Liz's letter to the council. He shared the essence of his phone conversation with Liz, including her willingness to pay back the money she had taken from the church. He asked for reactions.

"Did she give any reason for her actions?" Fred Wilson inquired.

Howard thought back to the phone conversation, "She said something about resentment toward the pastor. But she didn't elaborate."

Paul Walker felt it was time to open up with the council. The first thing he said was, "I have been doing a lot of praying." Slowly Paul shared that he had been feeling Liz's resentment for years. "Perhaps it was denial on my part that didn't allow me to recognize how severe it was. I felt she didn't like me, but I have never confronted Liz Sterling directly about her feelings. Perhaps I should have. I've been asking myself, could I have done something to prevent Liz's foolish actions?"

"Don't be too hard on yourself, Pastor," Bonnie said, feeling protective.

"Thanks, Bonnie, but . . . I wish I had seen this coming."

"So what kind of action are we going to take against her?" Darrel, always a man of action, asked the question on everyone's mind which no one wanted to address.

"I've said it before, and I'll say it again," Fred Wilson quipped, "let's not be hasty in our reactions. Why don't we give it some time? Give Liz a chance to make amends . . . see if she follows through with re-paying the church."

"I'd second that," Paul added. "I am just so relieved to have the monkey off MY back. And let's not forget, we are a church. We're in the forgiveness business, right?"

"Isn't there an old saying about adding insult to injury?" Jana asked. "My guess is that Liz is feeling pretty injured right now, so let's not add insult on top of it."

"Fred's counsel is wise, as usual," Howard responded. "Pastor Paul, Bonnie, Darrel, Jana, thank you. Thank you all for your participation in this difficult proceeding. Thank you for your wisdom, your patience, and your faith in God. I believe God's Spirit is at work here. With the council's consent, we will not bring any legal charges against Liz Sterling at this time. And let us hope it will never come to that. We will continue to pray for her, for our church, and for our pastor. The meeting is adjourned."

Members left the room, quietly mumbling good-night to one another.

22

The bitter cold had not broken since before Christmas. Temperatures had not gone above freezing for three weeks. The disturbing incident over the Discretionary Fund was put behind them when Liz Sterling sent a check for the amount she had embezzled from the church. A request for a transfer of their membership was included with the check. The council agreed not to prosecute. Liz and Phillip Sterling never returned to Trinity. As Paul prepared for Christmas Eve worship he felt as thankful as he ever had. The Christmas message of "Peace on earth, Good will to all" seemed to Paul, more real than ever.

Paul drove over the bumpy ruts in the packed snow and ice of the church parking lot. He saw Carol's car in its usual spot and was thankful she was willing to put on the coffee pot each morning. He was thinking about Liz Sterling. He also had Reiner and Tillie Holtz on his mind. He had seen them briefly at worship on Christmas Eve, but didn't get a chance to visit. They had left as soon as worship ended. He glanced up at the cross, glad to see it wasn't leaning. Paul said a silent prayer, watching the steam flow with each breath, and entered the building. He hung his coat in his office and greeted Carol. "Hi, Pastor, you just missed a call from Darrel Thomas. He said he'd like you to call him at home when you get time."

"Thanks, Carol," Paul smiled and poured his coffee. "Sure is cold out there."

"I heard a weather forecast that said it was going to warm up . . ." Carol paused . . . in June!"

"The way this winter is going, I wouldn't bet on it," Paul replied.

Paul called Darrel and they exchanged greetings. Darrel mentioned how lonely it was around the house without Francine.

"How long has it been, Darrel, two years?"

"Not quite, Pastor. Sometimes it seems like yesterday, and sometimes it seems like ages ago. I sure miss her."

"I'm sure you do. It must be hard."

"I am thankful for the Immigration Committee. I've enjoyed working with your wife and Chuck Kushman. Did you know he's got me ushering every other month now?"

"That's great! I hope you don't mind doing it that often. I always enjoy seeing you at the back of the sanctuary with bulletins for everyone."

"No, I don't mind at all. And I've enjoyed working with Maria Olivera. I get a real kick out of her! She really helped us understand why the Arriagas are attending St. Mary's. I'm glad she's on the committee."

"Speaking of the Arriagas, I haven't seen them since Thanksgiving. Have you spoken to them? I wonder how they are doing?"

"Yes, in fact, that's one of the reasons I called. I ran into Carlos and Lolita and the kids at the grocery store the other day. They said they were doing fine, but they didn't like the cold. They asked how long winter would last here in Indiana. I told them there would probably be snow and cold weather until April, but then it would start turning nice. Little Juan, their youngest, said he doesn't mind the cold and loves when it snows!"

"How about school? Did you ask how the children are adjusting?"

"I didn't have to ask. Both kids were excited to tell me about their school and their teachers. Carlos and Lolita said they were very proud of their children. And before we parted, they said to say hello to the Lutheran pastor and his wife, and to tell you how thankful they are to Trinity for all the help we gave them last year."

"Thank you, Darrel, for the wonderful report. I really appreciate hearing about them, and I'm thankful the Arriagas are doing well."

"The other reason I'm calling is that it doesn't look like we'll be sponsoring another immigrant family this year, and I was wondering, do you have any other projects I could work on? If I don't stay busy, I go crazy missing Francine."

"You know, Darrel, there is someone in the congregation I worry about. I've been trying to think of someone who might have time to visit him more often than I do."

"Time is something I've got to spare, Pastor. Who is it?"

"Do you remember Reiner Holtz?"

"Reiner? Of course I remember the old German. He gave us a bad time about the Arriagas."

"Yes, yes, I know. But what you may not know is that Reiner was in the hospital for several months last year. He had kind of a nervous breakdown. He's been at home; however, other than Christmas Eve, he hasn't been coming to church." Paul hoped Darrel would forgive Reiner and be willing to visit. "I think he's ashamed of his past behavior and too embarrassed to come to church."

"Hmmm . . . Let me give it some thought, okay, Pastor?"

"Sure. Nothing urgent. His address and phone number are in the church directory if you decide you're willing to talk with him." Paul said a silent prayer, commending this to God. "And if you do visit, let me know how it goes."

"You bet, Pastor." Darrel didn't seem too upset about Paul's suggestion. Before hanging up, he replied, "You know, Pastor, sometimes God uses coincidences like this to make amazing things happen. I'll certainly pray about it."

"Thanks, Darrel. A blessed New Year to you."

A week later, Darrel found himself in Reiner's living room, watching Reiner pensively blowing pipe smoke into the air. Tillie brought two steaming hot cups of coffee. Both men said they would drink it black. Tillie decided to head back to the kitchen. She had spaetzel ready to drop into oil. Darrel explained to Reiner how the pastor had suggested he make a visit and get better acquainted. He wanted to avoid talking about the Arriaga family, so he talked about his work on the Building and Property Committee. He told Reiner the story of Trinity's cross, and how it had been leaning, and needed to be replaced a few years before he and Tillie joined the church.

Reiner laughed when Darrell told him about the garbage can on the steeple. Reiner seemed to be enjoying the visit, and after a brief discussion of his growing up in Nazi Germany, he told Darrel about his mental breakdown and hospitalization last year.

"Sorry to hear about that, Reiner. How have you been feeling since you got out of the hospital?"

"Pretty good, as long as I stay on my medications. I also went through a lot of counseling. That was costing us a lot of money, so I just go once a month now. It's amazing how much I've learned about myself."

"Good for you, Reiner. I imagine Tillie is happy for you also."

"Oh yah. Poor Tillie. I don't know how she put up with me all zese years. It's amazing how we think we know who we are, but I was blind to how I was behaving. I had 'trust issues.' I didn't really trust anyone . . . even Tillie, I suppose."

"It sounds like you've come a long way. As far as the church is concerned, I hope you know you are still welcome there. The people I know at Trinity are very forgiving. I think they would be very pleased to see the 'new Reiner,' if you know what I mean."

"Yah, yah, I suppose we should come back. I know God doesn't like for us to make excuses. And I think Tillie would like to go. I'll talk with Tillie."

"If you don't mind changing the subject, I was noticing that beautiful chess set on the coffee table. Do you play chess? I haven't played in years."

"Yah, yah, I've played a little. Tillie doesn't like to play anymore because I always win."

"Maybe you could give me a refresher course. Shall we start a game?"

"Yah, Darrel. I would like zat." Reiner pulled a chair up to the coffee table, moved his pipe and ash tray next to the chess board, and with a flick of his hand motioned for Darrel to make the first move.

Thus began one of the most treasured friendships in each man's life. Darrel came every week for his chess game with Reiner. They were pretty evenly matched, but who won didn't matter. The real blessing for each was the conversation. Each of them felt vulnerable; Darrel, because of his grief and loneliness, and Reiner, because of his hospitalization and his past. Their trust in each other grew steadily month by month. They reached a point where Darrel could talk comfortably about Francine and some of the personal intimacies of their married life. Reiner opened up about his childhood, his fears, his conspiracy theories, and his efforts to be more trusting of others.

During Lent, Pastor Paul noticed that Tillie and Reiner had returned to church on Sunday mornings. Reiner stood by the door with Darrel, greeting members and visitors, and handing them a Sunday bulletin. Tillie was free to visit in the church kitchen, making friends with several women her age. Maybelle Stewart, the cookie lady, took a special liking to Tillie and always gave her a hug.

Paul had a particular concern about Maria Olivera. She had received an upsetting phone call from Reiner about a year ago. Would she be uncomfortable seeing him at the door? Would he look her in the eye when he handed her a bulletin? Paul watched for signs, hoping Reiner and Tillie would be accepted once again. The big Easter miracle is the resurrection of Jesus. A small but similar miracle occurred at Trinity on Easter morning. Out of the corner of his eye, Paul saw Reiner bow slightly and smile as he handed a bulletin to Maria. She smiled. He said something. She laughed. The long, cold winter had come to an end.

PART 3

23

"Randy, slow down! You know it's not good for you to eat so fast." Cheri couldn't believe how Randy was devouring his dinner.

"Can't help it, Mom, I've got to get to the gym for warm-up before the game. Don't you know who we're playing tonight?"

"I know, I know, the Gary Indians who beat you last year."

"Yeah, but not this year! I'm starting this year; and I know we're better than we were last year."

"Is this the last game of the season?" his dad asked.

"Last home game, Dad. Next week we play the East Chicago Mustangs in East Chicago. That'll be our final game; unless we make the playoffs."

"I thought you guys slipped to third place in the conference. What are your chances of making the playoffs?"

"We've got to win both these games, and the Mustangs have to lose one of their final games for us to move into second place. So, if we beat them next week, we're in for sure."

"Mom and I will both be there tonight. We sure hope you win."

"I'm feeling really confident, Dad. And I really appreciate you guys always coming to my games. You're the greatest!" Randy gulped down the remainder of his milk and shoved back his chair. "I wish Chip was here too."

"He's pretty busy with his college classes, but I'm sure he'll be pulling for you," Cheri replied.

"One more thing," Paul added, "don't forget that elbow to the face last year."

Randy carried his dirty dishes to the sink. "That guy graduated, but they still like to play rough. Don't worry, Dad, I'm not gonna be intimidated."

"I don't want you to be; I just want you to watch for dirty play and be careful."

"Thanks, Dad. I will." With that, Randy was out the door.

When Paul and Cheri got to the gym that evening, the noise was deafening. "Is it my hearing or do these games get louder every year?" Paul asked.

"Maybe both," Cheri answered as they climbed to an open space in the bleachers.

"It's hard to believe Randy's a senior and will be graduating in June." Paul leaned close to talk above the noise of the gym.

"Our little boys have become young men," Cheri looked at Paul and grinned.

Paul leaned even closer and whispered, "I still love your dimples."

Cheri grinned again and pushed him away. "Watch the opening jump," she ordered.

Weston got the tip. The ball was passed to Randy who set up the first play. The Warriors worked the ball patiently. Randy set a nice screen for the forward who sank a ten foot jumper. The Gary Indians answered with a basket of their own. Randy had been right. Like the coach said, "The Indians are still a physical team."

Weston had a slight lead at halftime. Paul was nervous, so he climbed down the bleachers and found the men's room. As he came out, a burly stranger confronted him. "Hey, aren't you from Weston?"

"Yeah," Paul answered, "the Warriors look good tonight."

"Your kid is the point guard, right?"

Paul was uncomfortable with this guy's in-your-face attitude. "Yeah, that's my son, number one."

"Well, I saw him play last year. The kid's a wimp. Before this game is over, he's gonna be doin' number two in his pants."

Paul took a step to the side, starting to walk away, angry, but determined not to answer. The parental bully stepped forward, brushed against Paul's shoulder and walked into the restroom. Paul was relieved he was gone and headed back into the gym looking for Cheri. *It's no wonder some students think they can bully others when their parents set an example like that*, Paul thought to himself. He debated whether or not to mention the incident to Cheri and decided to keep it to himself.

The second half got progressively rougher, and as the fourth quarter went into the final minutes, the score was tied. Randy had played well and had the most points of anyone on his team. The coach called a time out and gave them some advice and encouragement for the final minutes of the game. Paul was very proud of his son's determination. Randy played hard and showed no sign of being intimidated. Cheri said a prayer that there would be no intentional fouls and that no one would get injured . . . on either team.

The score was tied with two minutes to play. The crowd in the gym was hysterical. Randy missed a three-pointer. The Gary Indians scored on their next possession and went up by two. With less than thirty seconds, Weston scored to tie the game again. The Warriors' center intentionally fouled the Indians' center who was not a good free-throw shooter. He made one of two, putting the Indians ahead by one. After a time-out, Randy brought the ball up court. The Indians double and triple teamed him, making it impossible to get off a shot. He passed to the other guard who was open, but he missed the three point attempt. The buzzer sounded and the game was over. And so was the dream of the Weston Warriors making the playoffs.

Paul and Cheri were quiet on the drive home. They were proud of their son. He would be home a little later. He needed time to work through his disappointment over the loss. When Randy did get home, they both told him how proud they were of him and the way he played. He thanked them and then headed to his room to do some homework, and lick his wounds.

It wasn't right. It wasn't fair. The Gary Indians shouldn't have won this year too.

*   *   *

A week later, on the following Friday night, at a packed gymnasium in East Chicago, the Weston Warriors, led by their point guard, Randy Walker, defeated the East Chicago Mustangs 63-58. Again, Randy was the high scorer for the night. It was great to end the season with a win!

Cheri and Paul were getting worried because he wasn't home at 10:30, but they remembered Randy had told them the coaches were treating the team to pizza back at the Weston High gym after the game.

A few minutes after eleven the door flew open. "Guess what?" Randy yelled enthusiastically.

"You won!" Cheri and Paul yelled in unison.

"Yeah, but coach announced some awards tonight too. I was ranked second among all the guards in the league! And . . . get this . . . we just heard, the Gary Indians got beat tonight which knocked them out of the playoffs too!"

"All right!" Paul gave Randy a high-five. "I know how you LOVE the Indians!"

"Right, Dad."

"Now we have two special 'Randy accomplishments' to celebrate," Cheri joined in.

"The win tonight and my award," Randy replied.

"There's still something else I've been saving this since this morning," Cheri said, holding an envelope out for Randy.

"What is it?" Randy asked as he grabbed the envelope. "University of Iowa?" Randy began ripping it open. It only took a few seconds for him to let out another whoop, "I've been accepted!"

"Congratulations!" Paul said, as he and Cheri moved in for a group hug.

"You know, Randy, what this means for your dad and me . . . ?

"I know," Randy answered dejectedly, "two kids in college . . . and double the expense."

"Yea, but it also means an *empty nest*. We'll have the house to ourselves!" Cheri smiled as she looked at Paul.

"You'll miss me when I'm gone!" Randy teased.

24

Kathy Stiletto felt a little silly sneaking into Trinity on Sunday morning. It had been six years since she had been in the church to talk about her wedding plans. She wasn't even sure why she was there. Perhaps because she needed God? She wasn't sure what she needed. Kathy left her four-year-old daughter Autumn in the nursery, and took a seat near the back of the church. She didn't want to talk to anyone, and she hoped the pastor wouldn't notice her. The first things she noticed when she sat down were the green banners on the pulpit and on the altar. She tried to remember what the pastor called those things . . . paraments? Green would have been fine for the wedding, but no, it had to be blue! She tried to put all that wedding stuff out of her mind, but sitting here in church, it was impossible.

That had been a catastrophe! Andrea's minister said we didn't need a rehearsal. That should have been my first clue. Then, the afternoon of the wedding, he showed up at the hall twenty minutes late! Kevin's buddies had three or four beers down by then. The minister apologized for being late, hurried through the ceremony, asked for his check, and dashed out. The dinner was cold when it was finally served. The band showed up on time; but they had trouble with their sound system, blew a fuse or something in the hall, and all the lights went out for several minutes. After they got the power back on, the band started playing, and Kevin and I had the first dance. Then everyone started dancing with everyone else. All of a sudden, the lights went out again. When they came back on, I looked over at Kevin, and he and Andrea were all over each other. I couldn't believe my eyes! Kevin had this stupid look like he'd been caught with his hand in the cookie jar . . . Andrea's cookie jar. I stormed over and gave them both a piece of my mind! Andrea left the hall crying. Kevin apologized and said he probably had too many beers. We danced for an hour or so, and then people started leaving. You know how little girls dream about their wedding day? Well, my wedding day was a nightmare!

Kathy sat there in church praying, as the congregation sang and prayed. Somebody read from the Bible, and the pastor read the Gospel, and everybody stood up for that. When the pastor finished reading, everyone sat down again, and the pastor did his sermon.

While the pastor preached, Kathy's thoughts returned to her wedding. *Kevin and I argued a lot on our honeymoon. He said I changed. He said ever since I saw him kissing Andrea, I'd become a jealous bitch. I said he changed. He used to be so sweet; he'd do anything to please me. But after the wedding he said he was tired of being bossed around, and he wasn't going to take orders from no woman. We made up for a little while, but then we'd argue again.*

After the honeymoon, things got better for a while. Kevin went to Community College for a year and I continued working at Wal-Mart. After a year and a half at the local college, he told me he wanted to go to Ball State in Muncie. I said, why Ball State? And he said it had the kind of curriculum he wanted . . . but the way he said it sounded lame to me. So we argued about it for several weeks. "Why can't you go to Indiana University Northwest in Gary?" I begged. He sort of agreed and we sort of made up again. I guess it was then that I got pregnant, and he finished his second year at Community College.

First, Kevin made fun of me 'cause I got so fat. What was he thinking? Pregnancy would make me thin? He really hurt my feelings, so I got pretty bitchy again. Next thing I know, Kevin says he's leaving for Muncie. He left for Ball State in September, and I told him I'd come after the baby was born. I hated to change doctors and all that. He drove back to Weston on weekends. When my labor pains started, I called Kevin and he cut classes and drove back that day. My girlfriend took me to the hospital, but thank God, at least Kevin got there in time for the delivery. I delivered a beautiful baby girl. We decided to name her Autumn, 'cause she was born in the fall. Isn't that a pretty name?

When the baby came, he said it stunk so bad he wasn't ever gonna change them stinky diapers. I couldn't believe it! I said, "Kevin, what did you expect?" I tried to get him to do it, but he just refused.

A few weeks after Autumn was born, I got a friend of mine to watch the baby. Not Andrea of course; I hadn't seen her since the wedding. Things were pretty busy at Wal-Mart, with the holidays coming, so they wanted me to come back and work in the women's department. The manager there likes me a lot. I started working there in high school. She increased my hours and let me work 9 am to 9 pm three days a week. I was thinking about Kevin's attitude about the baby, so I told Kevin I'd come to Muncie when they cut my hours after the first of the year.

Right before Christmas, Kevin was studying for finals. I tried to call at his apartment but it seemed like he was never there. When he finally called me back he said he'd been studying a lot at the library. He told me his last final was on Friday and he'd drive home that night to Weston. I don't know why, but I had a funny feeling something was wrong. I called the University office and asked about the final exam schedule. They told me all finals would be finished on Wednesday. Then I knew for sure Kevin had lied to me.

I worked at Wal-Mart, Saturday, Monday, and Wednesday, and asked my friend to please watch Autumn on Thursday because I had some shopping to do for Christmas. I got up early Thursday morning and drove to Muncie. I knocked on Kevin's door a little after noon. I admit, I listened at the door for a minute before knocking, and I was pretty sure I heard a woman's voice inside. After I knocked I heard Kevin shout, "Just a minute, Barry." As he opened the door, he said, "Did you bring the videos I . . . ?" He stopped in mid-sentence, surprised to see me. I looked over his shoulder, and who stood there watching us? It was Andrea.

"Hey, Kathy," she said coolly. "C'mon in." Kevin was still speechless. He stepped back, and I walked in and stood in front of Andrea. I've never

been so angry in all my life. *"Don't get upset;"* she said, *"Kevin and I were just studying for our last final."*

"Your last final was yesterday," I said.

I wanted to kill both of them. I turned around and walked past Kevin without saying a word. I went out the door and walked toward the car. Kevin stood at the door and kept saying, "Kathy! Kathy, wait! Kathy, please, let me explain!"

I drove back to Weston, screaming and crying all the way home. I picked up Autumn at my friend's, and told myself I had to keep it together for her sake. I've been working at Wal-Mart to pay the rent, pay the baby-sitter, and buy food and diapers. Last month I had to take Autumn to the doctor for a terrible red rash all over her body. The medicine was really expensive, and I got behind on the rent, but at least the rash is gone. Now I've got a bill from the attorney for filing the divorce papers, but I don't know how I'll pay for that! And if all this weren't enough, my department manager told me this week that because sales were declining this summer, she would have to let someone go. I pleaded with her and reminded her about Autumn. She said she wasn't letting me go; it was the new girl. I breathed a sigh of relief, and then she said, "I'm sorry, but I will have to cut back on your hours." My life is a total disaster!

They're passing a brass tray for something and people are putting envelopes in it. Oh, I'll bet it's the collection for the church. Shit, I haven't got time to open my purse and it's empty anyway. Hand the tray to the next person and smile!

What am I doing here anyway? Do I really think God is going to help me? God's busy listening to all these other people and their problems; how can He do anything about the mess I'm in? Hey, God, remember me, Kathy Stiletto, like high heel shoes? I could really use some help.

For the remainder of the service, Kathy thought about how she used to yell at her mother to get her way, and how she could act cute and sweet with her dad to get her way. She thought about Kevin and how she used to yell at him; and if that didn't work, she would switch to cute and sweet.

Now there was no one to yell at, no one to flirt with, no one who would do what she wanted. She wanted to scream and yell at God, but realized it probably wouldn't do any good. People were singing the closing hymn. She would slip out the door before it was over, pick up Autumn from the nursery, and head for home. She thought of Autumn, so cute and sweet . . . sometimes . . . Autumn could yell and scream too.

25

Kathy Stiletto was in church again the following Sunday. She had picked up her check from Wal-Mart on Friday, cashed it, and paid several past due bills. There was a little left for groceries on Saturday, and a total of seventeen dollars and some change still in her purse. She left Autumn in the nursery and sat unobtrusively at the back of the church. Pastor Paul stood in the chancel and looked around as he shared a welcome and announcements. *Oh my God, he looked right at me! I hope he didn't recognize me. I hope he doesn't remember the wedding meetings.*

Pastor Paul did recognize Kathy, and he did remember the wedding meetings. But he quickly decided it was best to look the other way. He would greet her warmly at the door after the service. *If she says something personal, fine; if not, I'll just smile and say nothing, except welcome to Trinity.* Although he wondered what brought her back to the church, he didn't want to open any old wounds. The service began, and again Kathy had trouble focusing on the songs and liturgy. Too many personal problems continued to swirl in her mind. As luck would have it, or perhaps, as God would have it, Pastor Walker's sermon was on the topic of marriage. It was another of his poetic sermons. With the opening verses, it drew Kathy in.

Jim Bornzin

Two before the altar stand,
Pledge their vows, hand in hand,
Trembling with love, excitement, fear,
Together, drawing ever near.

"I now pronounce you husband and wife;
Health and happiness to you in this new life."
Each looks so young and clean and fresh,
Jesus says the two become one flesh.

Radiant, glowing, down the aisle,
To greet each guest with joyful smile.
Gown and gifts and rings and cake,
These and more a wedding make.

Good wishes from friends near and far,
For luck; a wish upon a star.
The wedding day is almost done,
But married life has just begun.

Now it's off to honeymoon,
The day that couldn't come too soon.
Weather cold, or weather hot,
In love, insane, it matters not.

Going home or distant places,
Hometown folks or foreign faces.
Just to hold you, feel you near,
Take your hand or shed a tear.

Laughing, dancing away the hours,
Just for now, the world is ours.
Children off to pursue a dream,
Following the Lord's most ancient scheme,
That as two lives are joined as one
Life's deepest lessons have just begun.

"The honeymoon is over,"
A proverb so true
That its' meaning keeps unfolding
All our life through.

It's back to work, or back to school,
For too short a time we played lovesick fool.
Bills must be paid, expectations increase,
Responsibilities mount, we yearn for release.
A baby arrives; our hearts swell with pride;
And so for a time, our anxieties hide.

But why does he do this?
And why does she do that?
Why does this partner look
So skinny or so fat?

Why is there always
A mess every day?
I don't remember the honeymoon
Being this way!
The wedding pictures hardly look real
Considering how I presently feel.

Reality, rediscovered, perhaps at a year,
Maybe less, or more, it begins to appear
That the dream we were living
In which we both kept on giving
Is becoming a task
As we both start to ask
For more than we give.
It gets harder to live,
And we pray to restore
Our oneness once more.

Now, snow is falling,
And each of us keeps calling
In subtle ways for what we need
Which the other person sees as greed.
One needs closeness, the other space;
Both stand in need of God's sweet grace.

A silent winter both agree,
For love's sake though we disagree,
Under the covers hurt is swept
And shameful thoughts in secret kept.
So day by day we grow apart,
Each harboring an aching heart.
We've prayed and we've tried,
And oh, how we've cried.
We've offered our prayer,
O God, aren't you there?

The winter is long, the winter is bleak,
We try to go on, even though weak.
Then comes a day, some crazy dumb thing,
A crisis occurs, the beginning of spring;
But all we can see is the damage that's done,
A dream that has crumbled, no victory won.

Now the anger comes forth,
Can't hold back any more,
A torrent of frustration,
Bitterness galore.
God brought us together,
But where is God now?
Where's the joy that was ours
On the day of our vow?

There comes a time
To consider divorce,
The answers have certainly
Not come by force.
And so the thought,
Once it crosses our mind,
Seems to offer an out,
The freedom to find
The happiness we dreamt
Our marriage would bring
When on the right person
We slipped the gold ring.

The Pharisees debated
The wisdom of life;
They asked, "Is it lawful
To divorce your wife?"

Jesus said, "Yes, it is lawful;
And yet, it is awful!
It's not meant to be,
But God made you free,
So provision is sent
If you cannot repent.
Some people have
Such hardness of heart
There is no other way
Except to depart.

Yet you need not despair
For God's love is still there
And is offered to each
In spite of the breach,
That new life might begin
In spite of the sin."
And in spite of the loss
That's why Christ died on the cross,

So that deep in the night
You might still have the light,
That together or apart
Love might return to your heart.

Divorce was never meant to be.
It always is a tragedy.
And yet as long as hope abides
Possibility for love resides.
If in humility, both seek God's will,
Forgiveness can lead to deeper love still.

Out of the ashes, Darkness and gloom
Can come a new life as though from a tomb.
Forgiveness is the key to the prisoner's release,
The key to new life, new hope, and peace.

The gospel of Jesus Is not ancient myth,
It's good news for all of the people we're with.
For wives and for husbands it leads us along,
Turning our darkness and tears into song.
It shows us our sin yet opens the way
For new possibilities day after day.

The winter is over, "Thank God," we sigh;
And so is the honeymoon, years have gone by.

The wedding photos faded, lie on a shelf;
We look into the mirror and see a different self.
For love has done its miracle,
The gospel's word is true,
This crazy person standing here
Is loved by God and you!

Love brought us together and
At times I've wondered why,
But trusting God and trusting you
Makes it okay to cry.
Love has led us through the years
Taught us with laughter as well as tears.
Forgiveness, patience, love, all do their part
In softening up our hardness of heart.

Our vows are renewed each day with a kiss.
In God's holy moments we taste of the bliss
Awaiting us fully in heaven some day
Where God's awesome love
Forever holds sway.
How blessed we are
To have a good mate,
What God has joined together,
Let no one separate. Amen

Kathy sat in the pew frantically wiping tears from her eyes. Her marriage had been a tragedy. It had ended in divorce. But Pastor Paul said, "You need not despair, God's love is still there." And what was that other verse? "Out of the ashes, darkness and gloom, can come a new life, as though from a tomb." *What are these tears?* she asked herself. *Tears of hope?* Digging into her purse, she pulled out her cosmetic mirror to check her makeup. Her face was red. She carefully wiped her mascara. She didn't notice the other visitor, also near the back of the church, in a pew across the aisle.

Mike Greenwood couldn't take his eyes off the young woman sitting one pew ahead of him and across the aisle. He watched her wiping her tears and checking herself in the mirror. Mike was still working for Napa Auto Parts, but when he got promoted to shift manager, he asked the guys to call him Mike instead of Michael. He had trouble focusing on the prayers as the service continued. Too many memories from high school were racing through his mind. It looked like Kathy was alone. *I wonder if she and Kevin the Quarterback are still together. I wonder if she remembers me. Hey, God, I know there are a lot of other people asking for your attention, but do you remember me, Michael Greenwood? I think I'm still in love with Kathy Stiletto. Should I try to talk to her? I'm not sure what to do. I could use a little help here.*

Mike made up his mind. He would follow her out of church, and talk to her, and ask her how things were going.

26

Carol Van Schoyck had been the church secretary for twenty years! Paul had recently given her the title of Administrative Assistant, but she couldn't get used to the "fancy title." Somehow it felt too ostentatious. Suddenly, it was all coming to an end. Carol's husband received a nice promotion from his publishing company, and he was starting his new position June 1, 2002. Unfortunately, his new office would be in Chicago, and that was too far to commute. Carol agreed she would quit her job at Trinity and they would move.

The council accepted her resignation in April. Paul was understandably sad. She was the hub of everything that happened at Trinity. She was trustworthy, a rock. She was, even Paul had to admit, as fussy about details and accuracy as he was. Her twenty year tenure made her an invaluable source of background information about members. His confidence was shaken as he tried to imagine doing his ministry without her.

The pastor suggested that Pentecost would be a nice day for Carol's farewell. It was one of the major festivals of the church year and attendance would be good. Everyone traditionally wore red for Pentecost Sunday. Carol wore a white blouse, white slacks, and a solid red wool jacket. Paul ordered a corsage of red roses. Carol was so glad that her husband, Bill, was able to come to church with her for the farewell reception. He didn't come very often. When he did, he told Carol he felt like a "fifth wheel." Everyone loved Carol; hardly anyone knew Bill.

On Sunday, Pastor Paul spoke about the Holy Spirit coming to the disciples at Pentecost. He said we should remember how the early church was blessed with gifts of the Spirit of God. Then he talked about the gifts God continues to give to today's disciples for the building up of the body of Christ.

"There is one gifted disciple with whom I have been privileged to work for the past seven years," Paul proclaimed. Carol felt embarrassed. She knew he was going to start talking about her. "God has blessed this special servant with friendliness, helpfulness, organizational skills, and typing skills. She is a confidence keeper, a trusted partner in ministry. And she tops it all off with a wonderful sense of humor! Carol Van Schoyck, would you please stand up?"

The congregation began to applaud. Carol stood, her face flushed with embarrassment. It seemed they would never stop clapping. "The mission of Christ's church here in Weston has been blessed with the gifts of the Holy Spirit through people like Carol," the pastor continued. "I hope everyone will stay for Carol's farewell reception after church today." Carol sat down and Bill reached over and squeezed her hand.

When the service was over members of the congregation made their way to the basement for Carol's reception. Before Carol and Bill reached the stairs, they were greeted by Mike Greenwood. "I just wanted to say good-by," Mike said in his nervous, self-conscious way. "It was nice getting to know you."

Mike had been coming to church alone, but pretty regularly for nearly five years. He liked the people at Trinity, and they seemed friendly, but he never hung around long enough to make friends. He liked the pastor's message; that was the main reason he came. "Well, I hope you like Chicago," Mike added as he headed for the door.

At the reception, there was a special cake in Carol's honor. "Twenty years of service" was written in red frosting on white; and below that was her name, Carol. One of the choir members came up to the microphone and sang a special song she had composed for her. Carol felt so honored!

Cheri gave her a big hug and thanked her for being such a great support to her husband. "I know he has placed a lot of trust in you, and you've never let him down. He's going to miss you a lot."

"Cheri, you're so sweet. Your husband has been a wonderful boss. He's treated me with such respect. It feels good to know you're trusted, and I hope I've lived up to it. I don't think I'll ever find a job I'll enjoy as much as I have working here at Trinity!"

"Do you think you'll look for employment when you get to Chicago?" Cheri asked.

"Not right away. I'll take some time to get our house settled, then maybe I'll look for something."

They hugged again and parted. Elmer and Arda Johannsen were waiting to say their good-byes. Carol couldn't count how many members came up and wanted their picture taken with her. It was an amazing day!

Bill and Carol Van Schoyck spent quite a bit of time in Chicago the next week or two looking for a new house. She had such mixed feelings. She kept thinking about how comfortable they were in their home in Weston, and then she'd get excited about a new, bigger house in Chicago. They agreed they wanted an older home, not a brand new place in the suburbs. Their daughter, who lived in Pennsylvania, said she had mixed feelings too. She had grown up in the house in Weston. She said it just wouldn't feel like "coming home" to a different place in Chicago. Their son-in-law reminded her it isn't the house that makes it home. It's the love you feel when you're with your family.

When Carol finally got her new home and address, she made sure Pastor Paul would send the Trinity newsletter each month. She was happy to read in June that they had hired a new secretary.

*   *   *

Hey! My name's Jeannette Brownlee. I'm the new office person here at Trinity. Whew! There is so much to learn. I'll just never get all the names right! Every time the phone rings here in the office, I grab the picture directory and try to find the picture that goes with the name.

I'm thirty-two, and I was raised in the Episcopal Church. My partner Kat and I have been together for four years. We had our union blessed at Saint James Episcopal Church four years ago. I've been a little reluctant to talk about our relationship. I suppose everybody knows by now; you know how fast word travels in churches. I was perfectly open with the interview committee, and I guess it didn't upset the pastor or committee too much or they wouldn't have hired me.

People have been really friendly! They usually say stuff like, "We just loved Carol! You're so much younger! We hope you'll like working here in the office at Trinity." Kat said she'd just stay at St. James; at least until we were sure this new job was working out. When I got the position as secretary, I started coming here to worship on Sunday mornings to get better acquainted. Kat says her daughter has friends in the Sunday School at St. James. I guess that's why she won't come to worship here. Lately, I've been going back to St. James every other Sunday, just so we can be together as a family.

I like Pastor Paul too. He's been really helpful, and he keeps reassuring me that he doesn't expect me to know everything in the first month or two. I'm surprised that Trinity doesn't have a website yet. I think I'll tell the pastor I could set one up if they want me to. I'll wait until I'm more familiar with the church and leaders and schedules and everything.

I asked the pastor if any members were having trouble accepting me because I'm a lesbian. He said, "Jeannette, just remember, especially for older folks, some of the changes that have taken place in society are hard to accept. Just give them time to get to know you."

27

Cheri and Paul weren't great aficionados of the arts, but their friends, Donna and Carl, insisted that they meet them at Visionary Gallery. Carl Webster was the new pastor at the Methodist church in Weston, and Donna had met Cheri at her husband's installation service. One of their Methodist church members was having a showing of her watercolors, so they invited Paul and Cheri to the gallery.

After supper Paul wanted to sit and read the newspaper, but Cheri reminded him they had an obligation. They arrived at the gallery a little after seven. A table was spread with punch and wine bottles, a variety of crackers and cheeses, plastic cups and plates. They weren't really hungry, so Paul poured a small amount of wine for Cheri and himself. They spotted Carl and Donna in the corner speaking with friends, and wandered over, being careful not to interrupt.

Donna saw Cheri coming their way and called out her name, "Cheri! How nice of you to come!" Paul shook hands with Carl. "Cheri and Paul, I'd like you to meet Janet Rasmussen, tonight's featured artist," Donna said as the Walkers shook hands with Janet. "Paul is the pastor at Trinity Lutheran Church and Cheri is becoming a very dear friend."

"So nice to meet you," Janet replied. "Donna and Carl have been so supportive. I can't believe the turnout tonight! I feel so honored. I hope no one is disappointed in my art work."

"How could they be?" Carl asked. "It is absolutely beautiful!"

The Walkers wandered through the gallery for about half an hour admiring Janet's watercolors. Cheri's favorites were the bright flower paintings, not still-life arrangements, just the flowers, often against soft, subtle backgrounds in shades of green. Carl and Donna were caught up in conversations with other Methodist friends, so Cheri and Paul continued on their own. They rounded a corner into another area of the exhibit and ran into a familiar face; it was Jeannette, their office manager from Trinity.

"Well, hi, Jeannette!" Paul said. "How nice to see you here tonight!"

"Hi, Pastor Paul! Hi, Cheri! I'd like you to meet my partner, Kat. I don't think you've met before, have you?" Jeanette's partner stared at Paul with a startled look on her face.

"Kat, this is Pastor Paul and his wife, Cheri."

Kat recovered quickly and reached out boldly to shake hands. "Umm, well . . ." Her mouth twisted to the side. "I met Pastor Paul . . . many years ago."

Cheri gave Paul an inquisitive look.

Paul looked away from Cheri and stared at Kat. "You're Kat?" he asked, "Kathy Stiletto?"

"Yup . . . I've been wondering how long it would be 'til you found out who Jeannette's partner was." Kat still seemed uncomfortable. She glanced at Jeannette and directed the next remark to her. "I guess that's another reason I've stayed at St. James."

"You two know each other?" Jeanette asked, puzzled. She looked at Cheri who was just as confused.

"If I remember correctly, you came to talk with me about a wedding." Paul looked from Kat to Jeannette and Cheri who were waiting for an explanation. "Many years ago . . . I don't even remember how many . . . Kat, who used to be Kathy, and her fiancé, came to my office to talk about getting married. To make a long story short, things didn't work out; so she got married somewhere else, I guess."

"Yup. I married Kevin Gianopoulis, but it didn't work out . . . neither the wedding nor the marriage!" Kat looked at Jeannette and shrugged her shoulders. "That's when I started going by Kat. When Jeannette and I made our commitment, I legally changed my name to Brownlee, like hers. So now I'm Kat Brownlee."

"You and Jeannette have been together for several years, if I'm not mistaken," Cheri said.

"Yes we have, about six years now," Kat replied.

"And you have a daughter?" Cheri questioned.

"Yes. I'm her birth mother, but I like to say WE have a daughter," Kat smiled at Jeannette. "Autumn is eleven and a half, almost twelve!"

"I hope we can meet her some day," Cheri responded.

"I hear about Autumn all the time . . . at the church office," Paul added, glancing at Jeannette.

"We're so proud of her;" Jeannette replied, "I can't stop talking about her. She calls me her *Other Mom*."

"Well, now that our little secret is out," continued Kat, "I suppose Autumn and I could come to Trinity with Jeannette once in a while."

"We'd love to see you there!" Cheri insisted.

"Anyway, it's nice to meet you, Mrs. Walker." Kat began pulling away.

"Likewise, Kat! And I do hope we get to meet Autumn," Cheri smiled.

"I'm glad we've met again, Kat," Paul added.

Jim Bornzin

"See you at the office on Monday, Pastor," Jeannette said as they moved away.

"Good night, Jeannette. Good night, Kat," Paul replied. "What a small world!" he said to Cheri. "You never know when you might run into someone from the past. I'm not sure I would have recognized her if she hadn't had such a startled expression when we came face to face."

"What was her name before?" Cheri asked.

"Kathy Stiletto. Can you believe it?"

"Ouch, and now she's Kat Brownlee," Cheri chuckled. "Quite a change."

"In more ways than one," Paul added.

28

"Gail was such a good sport about it!" Randy told his parents with amazement. "She didn't get mad or anything. I thought maybe she'd never want to see me again, but she invited me to her sorority party next Saturday."

It happened during Randy's senior year at the University of Iowa. His freshman year was devoted to basketball. He managed to qualify for the JV team; but judging by his performance, and knowing there were other guards who were playing on scholarships, he knew he wouldn't be back the following year. He decided to major in business during his sophomore year. One of the professors encouraged him in that direction and told him he had a lot of potential. His junior year was dominated by a series of girlfriend relationships, but nothing really worked out. He decided during his senior year he would devote himself to a strong academic finish. He wasn't really interested in going out or investing time in a relationship, until . . . until . . . Gail.

"This is the one," Cheri said to Paul when she hung up the phone. Paul had been on the extension in the bedroom.

"How do you know?"

"Something in Randy's voice . . . serious . . . but excited . . . and . . . I'd say he is 'smitten' but doesn't want to admit it to himself, let alone to us."

"But he said they only met a couple of weeks ago," Paul argued.

"Precisely. He's trying to convince himself that his feelings shouldn't be as strong as they are."

"Okay, okay, women's intuition and all that."

"All we can do is wait and see," Cheri concluded with a knowing smile.

Gail was always the first thing Randy talked about whenever he called. Then he would mention his finals or his grades, or his plans to come home for a weekend or holiday. Three months later, during his Christmas break at home in Weston, Randy told his parents he had to pick up a last minute gift for Gail. He didn't say a word when he got home; but that night, he sat at his desk studying the sparkling engagement ring. He rehearsed the proposal and couldn't wait to get back to college to see Gail.

The second week in January, Randy called to tell his parents he was engaged. All he heard at the other end of the phone was laughter.

"What's so funny?" he asked.

"Your mom was right," his dad answered. "Three months ago, the first time you called and mentioned her, your Mom said Gail was the one!"

"I guess Mom knows me pretty well," Randy replied.

"She certainly does," his dad agreed.

Randy told his parents he wanted to be married, the sooner the better. But Gail was only a junior and she really wanted to finish and get her degree. Randy confessed that it was really hard to wait.

Randy came home for Spring break, and couldn't stop talking about Gail and how hard it was to be away from her. He told his parents he wanted to get married when he graduated, but Gail wanted to wait until her graduation a year later. Cheri agreed that getting her degree was important for Gail. She reminded Randy, "The best things in life are worth waiting for."

Sometimes on weekends, Randy drove one hundred miles west to Des Moines to see his grandparents. Paul's parents had retired and were living in Des Moines. They were always delighted to see him, feed him, and listen to his stories about college, his fraternity, his girlfriends, and finally his fiancé. They kept asking when he was getting married, and Randy kept telling them, "Not until Gail graduates."

In June of 2002, Paul and Cheri drove to Des Moines to pick up his parents, and the four of them went to the graduation ceremony in Iowa City. Chip was tied up with his job and couldn't get away. He apologized for not making it back for Randy's graduation. After the ceremony, Gail joined the family at a nice restaurant.

Randy had majored in business, and was anxious to get started selling insurance. Iowa Mutual offered him a position and some training while he studied for his insurance license. He started in one of the Des Moines offices, mentored by a senior agent. In the months that followed, Paul and Cheri enjoyed getting to know Gail. Like Randy, she was very comfortable to be around, and she already felt like one of the family.

They learned that Gail's parents were Missouri Synod Lutherans, who weren't too happy when Gail announced her engagement to an ELCA pastor's son. Gail attended church frequently with Randy, first in Iowa City, and later in Des Moines. She was far more liberal than her parents and was comfortable with the Evangelical Lutheran Church in America's more open communion and the ordination of women.

Shortly before Gail's graduation, she and Randy began meeting with the ELCA pastor in Des Moines to plan their wedding. June 21, 2003, was the big day. The church was packed with family, college friends, and co-workers. Gail was radiant! Randy was ecstatic! They were thrilled when Chip flew in from California.

Grandpa and Grandma Walker were excited too. Randy and Gail found a small house just four miles from them. Gail started decorating and was already talking about "the baby's room." Gail was such a nurturing woman; Cheri knew she would be a great mom. Trevor was born ten months after the wedding, and Joy was born two years later. Cheri and Paul were thrilled

Jim Bornzin

to have their first grandchildren, and they couldn't have been happier with their new daughter-in-law.

* * *

Paul was at another evening meeting at the church. Cheri finished putting the dishes into the dishwasher and turned it on. She dried her hands on a towel and stared absent-mindedly at the clock on the kitchen wall. With Paul gone and the television off, the house was quiet. Something was troubling her, but she wasn't sure why she felt anxious. Paul wouldn't be home for at least an hour, so she decided to take a stroll around the neighborhood. She stopped for a few minutes to talk with the next-door neighbors who had a son in college. It was dusk as she came back into the house and turned on the lights in the kitchen. For a few moments, she stood frozen like a statue, struck again by a thought or feeling she could not quite identify. Was it the stillness of the house? Paul was gone. Chip and Randy had finished college; Chip was working in California and Randy in Des Moines. She shook off the lonely feeling of solitude, turned on lights in the living room, and opened the newspaper.

Cheri read for a while, reviewed some local stories, and was about to lay the paper aside when a *HELP WANTED* ad caught her eye. "**Business Manager**: Weston City Library. Experienced office manager needed. Send resume to Weston City Hall, c/o Milton Lieberman, Councilman."

Cheri's heart began pounding. *This is it! This is the answer to a prayer I haven't even prayed!* Her mind began racing. *I've been so happy not working. Paul's loved having me at home. Chip and Randy enjoyed my attention during their high school years. It's been so good to be available for them day and night. But both boys are gone. I've been anxious without knowing why. I need something to do. I think I'm ready to go back to work.* She moved into the study, turned on the computer, and pulled up an old file.

Cheri was hard at work on her resume and a cover letter when Paul got home from his meeting. "What'cha doing, honey?" Paul asked as he stuck his head in the study which had formerly served as Chip's bedroom.

"Applying for a job," she replied confidently.

Paul knew Cheri seldom made hasty decisions. Apparently she had been thinking about this and had made up her mind. "Where're you planning to work?" he asked casually.

"City Library, I hope," she answered. "They're looking for a business manager."

"They'll never find a better one!" Paul smiled and turned to leave.

"Thanks, honey," Cheri responded without looking up.

29

Paul's family was growing; so was the church. Paul felt very blessed to have a continuous influx of new members, mostly from the neighborhood. Ministry groups had multiplied. Several leaders from the council kept asking Paul about calling another pastor. It was a big step for Trinity; and Paul wasn't sure he was ready for it. The congregation council was getting more and more excited as the idea grew. The budget for the year included salary for an assistant pastor for six months, July through December. The congregation was in good shape financially. Shortly after Easter, Paul called the new bishop, Troy Pierson. He explained their need for another pastor and told him about the congregation's discernment process. The bishop asked about salary range and recommended they interview seniors from the seminary.

With seminary graduation in May, Paul knew they had to move quickly. Candidates would soon be available; and they were excited to interview, and hopeful to receive a call which would allow them to be ordained. Trinity elected a call committee in May which began work on a position description for the new assistant pastor. They wanted someone who would work with youth and families. Paul's time had become more and more devoted to community organizations and congregational committees, in addition to the pastoral time required for hospital visits, baptisms, weddings and funerals.

Bishop Pierson gave the committee two candidates' names. One was a young man who had come straight through college and seminary; the other was a slightly older woman who had taught in public school for several years before going to seminary. Both were invited to Weston for in-person interviews. The young man from the Lutheran School of Theology at Chicago was very scholarly. He told the committee he was considering the possibility of going on for his doctorate. He presented himself well, but it was Barbara Lambert who made a real hit with the committee.

*   *   *

The call committee consisted of two women, two men, and Pastor Walker. Howard Bardwell's term had expired on the council, and he seemed a logical person to serve on the committee. At the first meeting, he was elected by the others to serve as chairperson.

Pastor Walker met Barbara at O'Hare airport in Chicago. She had flown in from Pennsylvania where she was attending the Lutheran Theological Seminary at Philadelphia, only eighty miles from her home in Allentown. "How was your flight?" Paul asked.

"Okay, I guess, but those airplane seats aren't made for wide bodies like mine," Barbara joked.

Paul guessed she was about five feet, three inches tall, and weighed over two hundred pounds, maybe close to three hundred. Barbara was neatly dressed and moved with grace for a person of her size. They walked to the baggage claim area to get her suitcase. While they waited, Paul asked about her seminary experience. With luggage in hand, Paul led her through the parking garage to his car and placed her bag in his trunk. On the two hour drive to Weston they got better acquainted, as they talked about their families. She also discussed her teaching experience in the Allentown public schools. Paul was impressed with her poise and maturity. When they reached Weston, Paul suggested they stop at Subway for lunch before the interview.

Paul gave Barbara a quick tour of the church before the interview began and told her about Trinity's history and mission. In the conference room Barbara shook hands with the others and took a seat with a file folder on her lap. She appeared both nervous and excited. "This is exactly the kind of church I was hoping for!" she told the members.

"Have you read our position description? And how does it fit with your interests?" Howard asked her.

"Yes, I've read it, and it fits exactly what I would like to do for my first call. As you probably know from reading my profile, I was a junior high school teacher for eleven years before going to seminary. I love teaching and I love working with youth."

"What made you decide to go to the seminary?" Jana Nygaard asked.

"I've been thinking about it for a long time. I was active in my home congregation in Allentown, teaching Sunday School, Vacation Bible School, and assisting in worship. Although I loved teaching in the public school, it was pretty much the same routine year after year. I saw the variety of things my pastor was called to do and began to wonder if God was calling me to parish ministry. I was basically a history teacher, but I wanted to learn more about the Bible. I wanted to learn more about the history of the Old Testament, and the early centuries of Christianity. Finally, I said to myself, 'Barbara, you're not getting any younger! If you're going to do it, why put it off any longer?' So I applied and was accepted."

"And did your seminary experience live up to your expectations?" Jana asked.

"Absolutely! The longer I was there, the more certain I was of God's call to parish ministry."

"What do you consider your greatest strengths or gifts for ministry?" Maybelle Stewart asked.

"My love for the Lord, Jesus Christ; my organizational skills; I like to plan very thoroughly and well in advance of events; and of course, my skills as a teacher."

"Would you consider yourself a Type A personality?" the chairperson asked.

"I suppose I am," Barbara admitted, somewhat reluctantly. "I'm pretty much a perfectionist and I tend to get upset when things don't go as planned."

"Thank you for your honesty," Howard replied. "You seem to be a most serious young woman."

"Very serious when it comes to my work; but I laugh and giggle a lot too."

"Tell us, Barbara, is there anything you'd like to share with us that you haven't told us so far?" Pastor Walker asked.

The candidate thought for a few moments and decided to share something very personal. "You remember how I said I felt called to the seminary. Well, there was one other factor that influenced my decision to go when I did. I had been going with another teacher for almost five years. He and I had a lot in common and I kept hoping he would ask me to marry him. When I finally asked him what he thought about marriage, I realized our views were very different. We kind of drifted apart after that . . . And that also prompted me to say 'If I'm ever going to the seminary, it's now or never!'"

The interview went on for another hour. Barbara continued to answer questions honestly, showing her love for the Lord, the church, and her calling. When the interview was completed, Howard Bardwell asked if she would like to stay for dinner. He and Sheila Gordon, the music director, took her to a local restaurant. The Call Committee asked Paul if he felt he could work well with Barbara, to which he replied positively. Little Maybelle, the cookie lady, commented on Barbara's weight and said she hoped it wouldn't become a health issue for her. Overall, the reactions were favorable, and all of them agreed she should be recommended to the congregation for a Letter of Call.

*   *   *

Barbara Lambert was very excited to share the news of her interview with her classmates and friends when she returned to the seminary in

Philadelphia. Her roommate asked her, "What was the pastor like? Did you like him?"

"Yeah, I think so. We had a good talk driving from the airport to the church," Barbara replied. "He seems like an okay guy; I'd guess he's in his fifties. He's been the pastor at Trinity for about twenty years."

"What about the church and the call committee?" another friend asked next.

"I liked the members of the committee; they were really nice. And I liked the church. Trinity is a good size, not too big and not too small. The urban setting should be interesting. Most of all, I got a bang out of Sheila! She's the Music Director. I think she and I could be very good friends. She is a hoot! She says whatever is on her mind, and she doesn't care what anybody thinks! Maybe I like that about her because I always wished I could be a little more spontaneous. Howard Bardwell said she is really talented and does a wonderful job with the choir and music program. I hope I get to hear their choir. In fact, I hope I get the call to Trinity."

"Do you think you will?" her friend asked, feeling Barbara's excitement.

"I feel pretty good about the interview. I think it went well. Now I just have to wait and see. All these years of preparation! I can hardly believe . . . I might be a pastor in another month or two!"

*   *   *

Barbara Lambert was recommended to the congregation and a vote was taken on the second Sunday following her interview. She accepted the call immediately and could hardly wait to get started. She was ordained on August 27, 2006, in her home church in Allentown, Pennsylvania, surrounded by family and friends. She spent the next two weeks planning her move to Weston. On the Sunday after Labor Day, Bishop Troy Pierson installed Barbara as the Assistant Pastor of Trinity Lutheran Church in Weston, Indiana. She was thrilled to hear the choir sing a special anthem, "Be Still and Know That I Am God." Watching Sheila direct the choir was like watching ballet. Sheila's every movement was filled with passion for the music.

At the reception following worship she met and talked with a number of council members. She sat at a table with a friendly elderly couple, Elmer and Arda Johannsen, who wanted to tell her all about Trinity and all about the wonderful friends they had here. Barbara was also pleased to get acquainted with Jeannette, the new parish secretary. They would be working closely together. Jeannette promised to help her in the long process of getting to know the church members.

Paul and Cheri Walker sat at a table with Carl and Donna Webster from the Methodist Church. After talking about their kids and grandkids, Donna asked Cheri how she liked her new job at the library. Cheri said she was enjoying it. "How about you, Donna, have you thought any more about looking for a job outside the home?"

"Yeah, I've been thinking a lot about it. It's been quite a few years since I worked in an office. I really don't have much in the way of computer skills. I would like to find something . . . just reluctant to apply, I guess."

"You know what? There's an opening at the Weston Public Library downtown. It's only part-time, but it may work into a full-time position. Do you think you'd be interested?" Cheri asked.

"Well sure, I'd be interested . . . but like I said, I'm not sure I'm qualified." Donna replied.

"You'll never know unless you apply," Cheri urged her friend. "You can use me as a reference."

"Gee, that'd be great. Maybe I will apply. Say, wouldn't it be fun if we worked at the same place? That way we would see each other every day. Wouldn't that be hilarious?"

"That'd be wonderful!" Cheri replied. "Why should our husbands have all the fun?"

"Oh, I can't wait to tell Carl!"

Two weeks later, Donna was working at the library. Pastor Barbara Lambert was teaching her first confirmation class. Paul was giving thanks for his new Assistant Pastor; and he was pleased that the call process had gone so well.

30

Palm trees. Warm winters. Chip could hardly believe he was living in California. Though he missed his parents and "little brother," he was "livin' the dream!" Chip graduated from Weston High School in 1995 and from Indiana University in 2000. At a job fair his senior year at IU he met a rep from Allied Business Systems in San Jose. They had a great conversation and Chip told him he was definitely interested in working for them. The rep gave his resume and a recommendation to the personnel department. And the next thing Chip knew, he was flying to their office in San Fernando, near L.A., for an in-person interview. He met with several department heads, and at the end of the day, they offered him a position.

As Chip explained later to his parents, "We do set-up and maintenance of computer systems for businesses all over the world. I've been to New York, Florida, Texas, Minnesota, and of course, here in California. So far, they haven't sent me overseas, but I think they will when I get a little more experience. Oh, and guess what? Everyone at work calls me 'Computer Chip!' Do you remember, Dad, you called me that when I declared my major? Well, I've been hearing it ever since. I've decided to embrace it; so I had it printed on my business card. At least clients remember my name!"

Cheri and Paul were glad he called home as often as he did. During the first few months he called almost weekly from his apartment in San Fernando. They could hear the excitement in his voice. "Mom, Dad . . . how lucky can one Hoosier get? I never dreamed I'd be living and working in sunny California! Don't get me wrong, I'm glad I went to Indiana University. I had great professors there. I'm glad I majored in Computer Science. Thank you both for all the support and encouragement you gave me growing up. But the weather here is unbelievable. Warm and sunny in the summer, warm and sunny in the winter! I can get to the beach at Santa Monica or Malibu in half an hour; and the mountains of the Angeles National Forest are just an hour east of here!"

"We're so happy for you," Cheri replied, "we just wish you weren't so far away."

"Well, you'll just have to come out and visit," Chip responded. So they did, making a trip out west each summer for the first three or four years. Chip was also making vacation trips back to the mid-west each year. Paul and Cheri were always glad to see him and hear about his work, his travels, his hiking, and occasionally about women he was dating. They really hoped he would find someone to marry, but they didn't want to be pushy.

Five years after Chip's graduation they got the phone call they had been hoping for.

"Mom, Dad . . . you won't believe what's been happening the past month or two. I've met the most fantastic woman! Linda and I met at her office when I was there doing some diagnostic testing on their computer system. She's a serious person, but sometimes she's really funny. She's super smart. Oh, and you won't believe this . . . she played the trumpet in high school!"

"It sounds like you two may have a lot in common," Cheri could hardly contain herself.

"I think you'll both be glad to know," Chip continued, "Linda is a good Christian; she was raised Catholic. She's into angels and meditation and Christian yoga. I'm not sure how this faith thing will work out, but I've gone to church with her some Sundays, and she's tried attending the Lutheran church with me."

Paul and Cheri were thrilled again to hear the excitement in his voice. "That's great!" Paul replied. "And don't worry too much about the religious differences. I'm confident that as mature young people, you'll work it out."

"Thanks, Dad, I was hoping you and mom would understand."

Chip and Linda went together for a year and a half before he finally asked her to marry him. The wedding was planned for March 27, 2007. Paul and Cheri, Randy and Gail, flew to California for the wedding which took place in the Catholic Church. The Walkers weren't upset; they were thrilled to meet Linda and her parents, sisters and brother. It was a beautiful wedding!

During the year following the wedding, Cheri waited anxiously to hear the news of a baby. Chip continued to talk about how much he was learning with Allied Business Systems, saying more than once how good they've been as an employer. Linda really liked her job and never mentioned anything about "starting a family."

When Chip finally shared their plans, in response to one of his mom's questions, he said simply, "We've decided to wait a few years before starting a family." Paul understood, but Cheri was a little disappointed. Chip told his dad, "Linda's parents weren't too happy either; they're . . . you know . . . old-school Catholics."

The summer after the wedding, Chip and Linda flew back to Indiana for a week, so Linda could see where Chip grew up in Weston. They also spent a few days in Des Moines with Randy and Gail, and visiting Grandpa and Grandma Walker. While they were there, a thunderstorm struck with such fury they thought they'd be washed away. The TV weather report showed where tornadoes had touched down in Kansas. It was hot and humid in Iowa; it was hot and humid in Indiana. They couldn't wait to get back to sunny, dry California. As far as Chip was concerned, he was "livin' the dream!"

31

Mike Greenwood dreamed of being a NASCAR driver some day. As he sat in church, Mike imagined himself speeding around the track listening to the roar of the powerful engine, watching the checkered flag wave over his car, and waving to the crowds of adoring fans as he held his trophy high! Mike knew it was only a dream. Maybe, if God was kind enough, his dream would be fulfilled in heaven. In the meantime, he was satisfied with his humble job at Napa Auto Parts. Maybe supplying parts was fulfilling enough, helping keep the cars of ordinary people running safely and reliably. Pastor Paul's sermon on humility reminded him that the arrogant and proud people of the world often need to be taken down a notch or two, to realize how fortunate they are.

Jesus said: "For all who exalt themselves will be humbled; and those who humble themselves will be exalted." Luke 14:11

"The honor of your presence is humbly requested
Please come for the dinner at eight."
I wasn't surprised by the invitation,
Everyone wants "Jimmy the Great!"

They'll probably ask a few words from each guest,
I've got a great speech on motivation.
I'll fill out this card and return it at once;
They'll be pleased I've made reservation.

Jim Bornzin

My career as a coach has taken me far,
Just look at this wealth that's surrounding,
The size of my house, my cars and my boat,
My success has been truly astounding!

Great coaching's a talent, a gift and an art,
So few have skills such as I.
Surround yourself with a good coaching staff
And the best players money can buy.

But you've got to make them believe they're the best,
I expect a lot from my players and get it.
I make them work hard, once they've tasted success,
I know they will never regret it.

So . . . last night was the banquet; I dressed in my best,
And arrived a little before eight.
I just don't believe in that society hogwash
About being "fashionably late."

I got out of my limo and walked through the door,
The hall was splendid, amazing,
The guests, a hundred or more, were milling about,
And each at the others was gazing.

I kept looking for someone familiar,
A coach or player I knew;
But no one I saw in the hall was a star
And slowly my confidence grew.

No Michael Jordan, no Tiger Woods,
No Harrison Ford or Bonnie Raitt;
No Sammy Sosa, no President Bush,
Just me . . . "Jimmy the Great!"

They've invited the fans, just their friends I presume.
I smiled my way through the hall,
Shook hands with my host, not meaning to boast,
Had no idea how far I would fall.

I took my seat at the head of the table,
The notes in my pocket were ready.
Slowly, the other guests took their seats
And our host with a voice clear and steady . . .

Introduced me to the person on my right.
"This is Nelson Mandela, reconciler of races,
Whom I suppose you've never met.
Would you mind exchanging places?

Embarrassed, but still smiling,
I moved one seat to the right.
And next to me now was a little old lady,
So frail and so very slight.

"Please say hello to Mother Teresa,"
Was the next thing my host said.
And so I traded seats again,
And slowly hung my head.

Looking to the right once more
I knew I'd met defeat . . .
"My name is Cesar Chavez."
So I moved another seat.

My host came back and spoke again,
"I know this may seem strange,
But this is Florence Nightengale
And you'll have to rearrange."

Guest by guest I moved on down,
As over each chair bending,
I was asked to move again
Through hours never ending.

I was near the bottom now, as low as I could go,
One last guest beneath me, a ragged, bearded bum,
With rumpled clothes and matted hair,
I'm down here with the scum.

My knees and hands were trembling,
Once again our host drew near,
He smiled reassuringly
As he sensed my foolish fear.

"I'd like you to meet my Son, the rabbi.
He understands your shame.
This is Jesus . . . Jesus of Nazareth;
I'm sure you've used his name."

To my surprise the hall was filled with laughter
As I began to cry,
The guests were laughing with the host,
At first I wondered why.

Then it all made sense to me . . .
I was such a puffed-up fool!
I had to fall . . . to learn humility;
I was invited to heaven's school.

The host was God, the bum was Christ,
I laughed until I cried . . .
And suddenly, I realized . . .
Last night . . . I up and died!

At the back of the church Mike shook hands with the pastor and told him it was a good sermon. As he walked to his car he realized that slowly, over the past few years, the church had become a kind of family. He was comfortable there. People seemed to accept him for the loner he was; nobody pushed for his participation and yet he always felt welcome. He used to think all Christians were judgmental, but as he became familiar with the Lutherans, it seemed they were willing to leave the judging to God.

His old Chevy started reliably. He did minor repairs himself, and it had at least a dozen Napa parts in it by now. Mike pulled out of the parking lot and headed for Lucky's Tavern. He smiled as he thought about his friends Charlie and Eddie and Ron . . . still another family. He wondered how many years Whitey had worked there behind the bar. He figured everyone called him Whitey because of his light blond hair, although it was disappearing rapidly, leaving a large shiny bald spot on top. Mike chuckled as he thought how much Whitey reminded him of a priest!

The glass brick windows allowed a little diffused sunlight inside, and provided privacy for the tavern customers. Mike walked in, headed toward the bar, and saw Whitey pouring a draft beer which he knew was meant for him. Charlie was already sitting at his usual bar stool, eyes glued to the big TV screen, as the announcer introduced the NASCAR drivers and their cars. Mike took the stool next to him and the two exchanged greetings. Mike picked up the frosty glass and took his first swallow of beer.

"How was church this morning?" Charlie asked, knowing Mike's routine.

"Nice as usual. The pastor had a great sermon! You know, I can't sing to save my soul, but I like listening to our choir; and sometimes, during the hymns I get kinda choked up."

"You old softie, you. Aren't there some good lookin' babes there you could get hooked up with?" Charlie asked. He turned to look at Mike and gave him a big grin.

"Very funny, Charlie. I've told you, some people are meant to be single. I'll be a bachelor as long as I live and I don't mind. A guy can only be hurt so many times and then he knows it's time to quit." Mike watched Whitey wiping the shiny bar top. The TV droned with a commercial about a law firm that helps you get paid after an accident. The unspoken connection to racing accidents was probably no coincidence.

Charlie stared at the TV, "I know whatcha mean."

"Besides, I'm a creature of habit. I'm a NASCAR fan. I love football. I like comin' down here to Lucky's; and if I was married, my wife wouldn't be too happy about my comin' here after church."

"You got that right. My wife used to fuss about my comin' down here to Lucky's on Sunday afternoon. She'd say she just couldn't understand how a bunch of grown men could enjoy watchin' a bunch of guys drive their stupid race cars around a track. I told her I work all week and Sunday afternoon is my time to relax and enjoy what I enjoy . . . racing . . . and football. Hey, I don't come home drunk, I told her, so quit complainin'! So she finally shut up about it."

Mike nodded with sympathy and understanding.

Mike Greenwood could nurse a beer through an entire afternoon. He wasn't an alcoholic, though he did spend a lot of hours at the tavern. Sometimes, when Eddie and Ron came in, they'd all sit at a table as close as possible to the big screen. They loved NASCAR racing; football too. Most weekends they could be found at Lucky's. The local pub had quite a few regulars; none more regular than Mike. As they sat watching race cars circle the track, Mike began talking about his past.

"Y'know, Charlie, I've seen some pretty sad drunks in my day."

"Yup, me too."

"The older I get, the more I think my mom . . . I mean, my birth mother . . . must have been an alcoholic."

"Why's that?" Charlie asked.

"Well, the state took me away from her when I was five and put me in foster care." Mike took a small sip from his beer. "All I remember about her was that she yelled at me a lot. She said she loved me. She would be real sweet and huggy sometimes; but she smelled bad and I would pull away."

"Was she a smoker too?"

"Yeah . . . always had one lit. And lotsa times when I wanted to play, she'd be asleep on the sofa in the middle of the day."

"No doubt about it, Mike. She was a home-bound drunk."

"Guess that's why I can't stand more than a beer or two. I never wanna get like that."

"Me neither."

"And as for never getting married . . . ha! I've learned my lesson." Mike lifted his beer and set it back down without drinking. "Did I ever tell you that story?"

"Can't say's you did."

"Well, it all started when I was in high school. Fell in love with this girl named Kathy, Kathy Stiletto. Honest to God, that was her name. Well, she dumped me for another guy. He was the quarterback on the football team; but he was a jerk. I thought when we graduated Kathy and I would get married. But she married him instead . . . She married the jerk . . . Broke my heart."

"Aw, Mike. That kinda thing happens to every guy."

"Wait a minute, Charlie, I'm not done yet. She marries Kevin what's-his-name. So I try to forget about her. Several years later I'm sitting in church and guess who shows up?" Mike turns to look at Charlie. "Yup, Kathy Stiletto . . . but now she's Kathy what's-her-name. I get to talking to her after church, and sure enough, she and Kevin have split. Not only that, but she's got a kid."

"Don't tell me . . . you got back together with her?"

"Exactly." Mike takes another sip of beer. "Remember, I was raised in foster homes. More than anything, I wanted a real family . . . like my friend Brian's. I swore if I ever got married, it would be forever. And I'd be a real dad. And I'd give my kids what I never had."

"A real family."

"Right. So I wasn't too happy that there was this kid who was really Kevin's. But then I thought, this kid, her name was Amber . . . no, Autumn; she needs a good family. And Kathy and I could have our own kids once we got married. Working for Napa wasn't the greatest paying job in the world, but hey, it was steady; and I didn't have a college degree or anything. God was giving me a second chance with Kathy. Seemed like a dream come true."

"Then what happened?"

"We were seeing each other pretty regular. I was pushin' to get married, but she kept pullin' away. I could understand why she was hesitant. The jerk, Kevin, had been two-timing her and it broke her heart. I could see she never wanted to be betrayed again. I told her I knew how it was; I had my heart broken once and I'd never do that to her."

"So?"

"So after a year and a half, I bought a ring and got down on my knees and I asked her to marry me; and she said she just couldn't. She said, 'You're real sweet, Mike, but I just feel suffocated when I'm around you.' It was like havin' a dagger stuck in my heart . . . again."

"Aaaw, man! . . . So that ended it?"

"Yeah, my big second chance . . . up in smoke."

"Man, that's rough."

"That's when I swore 'Never again!' Whenever I see a pretty girl I get this terrible pain inside. When I was in high school pretty girls made me nervous. This is different. It's like a little voice in my head that says, 'Don't even think about it.' Like I said, some people are meant to be single."

"Tell me somethin' else, Mike. How come you're such a church-goer?"

"Like I said, Charlie, I'm a creature of habit; and I think that's one of my better habits. It's like this. When Kathy dumped me the first time, back in high school, I went to church a few times with my friend Brian. He used to tell me that going to church and talking to God helped him a lot. After graduation, Brian was working as a janitor in the church when some idiot broke into the building one night. Brian tried to stop him and ended up getting killed. We were all in shock. Anyway, I went to Trinity Lutheran for

Brian's memorial. I kept asking, 'God, how could you let this happen?' But I never got an answer.

"When Kathy dumped me the second time I was so angry at God! I kept asking, why? I went to church again. I wasn't praying TO God as much as I was praying AT God. 'How could you let this happen again?' I still hadn't figured out why God let Brian get killed. I started goin' to church real regular to see if I could get any answers about Kathy, and Brian; and to try and figure out what I was supposed to do with my life."

"Whoa! I never knew all that. So now you go to church . . . and then you come to Lucky's."

"Works for me." Mike and Charlie turned their attention to the television. "Hey, final lap." Mike pointed at the screen. "Looks like Johnson has another win!"

"I think Jimmie will take the championship this year for the third straight time! He's way ahead of Edwards in points." Charlie replied.

"Three years in a row? Won't that tie Cale Yarborough's record?" Mike asked.

"Yeah, but that was in the seventies when the competition wasn't nearly what it is now."

"Man, I love watchin' these races!" Mike lifted his glass and clinked it against Charlie's. "Here's to the champions!"

"I enjoy comin' down to Lucky's 'cause it gets so darn lonely around the house on weekends. I come down here and watch college games on Saturday, pro games or NASCAR on Sunday; AND I get to enjoy the company of DUMBSHITS LIKE YOU and Ron and Eddie!"

"What did you just call me?" Charlie asked in a loud voice. The two guys laughed so hard other customers turned to stare.

"Charlie, whatdaya say we split an order of ribs?"

"Sounds good to me."

"Hey, Whitey! Cook us up some ribs! And a big order of fries! And while you're at it, why don't you switch channels and see if the Colts game has started."

"Sure thing, Mike!" Whitey replied.

Slowly, through the years, God was helping Mike Greenwood find his family. It was not the traditional family with wife and kids, but a community of friends, in several places, at work, at church, and even at the tavern, where he was loved and given the opportunity to love and care for others.

"Y'know Charlie, some people are meant to be single. I'll be a bachelor as long as I live and I don't mind. By the way, did I tell you what the pastor asked me after church today?"

"No . . . you just said he had a good sermon."

"As I was shaking his hand at the door he said they were forming a new refugee committee for a kid from Iran. The story is he was put in prison in Tehran for becoming a Christian. Lutheran Immigration and Refugee Service asked our congregation to sponsor him and help him get settled here in the U.S. The pastor asked me if I wanted to be on the refugee committee."

"What did ya tell him?"

"Just said I'd give it some thought and prayer."

"Why don'tcha do it?"

"I might. I just might."

32

My name is Omar Shufti. I came

here from Iran. Let me tell you about Tehran; it is a beautiful city, the modern capital of Iran. There are over seven million people living in Tehran. That's nearly as many as there are in New York City. There are so many ancient mosques and churches; you wouldn't believe how old they are. Many tourists are familiar with the Azadi Tower which commemorates the 2,500th anniversary of the Persian Empire. Most Americans do not realize that Iran is such an ancient civilization. My family still calls it Persia sometimes. But my favorite site in Tehran is the new Milad Tower; it's magnificent. We have many beautiful universities. And the mountains! Our family loved to take drives into the Alborz Mountains just north of the city. They have snow on them much of the year. And to the south is the desert!

My family is Persian and Muslim. My father works for the government in the national transportation department. He works on highways, roads and bridges. My mother has raised four children. I am the second oldest son and I have two sisters. All of us have gone to college, even the girls. I was at the university when I met Jesus. We were having a discussion in the dormitory one evening and someone asked if I had ever read the Christian Bible? I told them, of course not. Then they asked if I would like to. I wasn't sure if I should answer truthfully because I knew it might be a trap. I don't remember exactly what I said, but later that night, one of my friends came to my room with a bible. He handed it to me through the door, gave me a sign not to tell anyone, turned and left.

That night, I read Matthew and Mark, and fell asleep before I finished Luke. I was struck by the wisdom of the prophet, Jesus, and I remained skeptical about some of his miracles. They kept calling him the Son of God, which I could not understand. Allah is one, and Mohammed is his prophet. This is what my family believes, and most of my countrymen. But Jesus seemed very wise, and very kind, and very compassionate. I was intrigued by his arguments with the Pharisees who seemed like the imams, the teachers of Islam.

A week or two later, my friend asked if I wanted to come to a secret meeting to discuss Jesus. I should have said No, but my curiosity was too great. I discovered the meeting was actually a Christian Bible study, devoted to the gospel and spreading faith in Jesus. I knew this was against the law, but I really wanted to learn more. When they explained how Jesus died for our sins, I realized there was nothing like this great love in Islam. The more I read the gospels, the more real Jesus became for me. I felt like one of his first disciples, willing to call him Master and Lord, and finally accepting the mystery in the gospel of John, that Jesus was the Word of God the Creator who became a human person and lived among us. There aren't three gods, as Islam says about Christianity; only one God, as Islam says. Yet the Christians say this one God is known in three different forms: as the Creator whom Jesus called Father, Jesus the Savior, and the Holy Spirit who is God's invisible, mysterious power and presence. After meeting with the Christians for a couple of months, I decided to be baptized, but I didn't tell my parents.

About six months after I began meeting with the Christians, one of the newer members of our group told the university officials about our meetings, and we were all arrested. I was held in prison for almost a month. I was questioned and constantly lectured about the truth of Islam and the Satanic lies of Christianity. Finally, with my parents pleading mercy from the court, I was released and warned never again to practice the abomination. With my name on record, I could be tried and executed if I was apprehended for publicly practicing the Christian faith. My parents begged me to give up my new faith, but I continued meeting secretly with my Christian friends.

One of them was very courageous in distributing Bibles. He was arrested and sentenced to a very long term in prison. My parents finally urged me to flee from the country and seek refugee status in Canada or the United States. I went first to an uncle who lived in India. I stayed with him for almost four months. Meanwhile, a friend of my father's spoke to one of his friends at the American embassy in Tehran, and soon my name was accepted for sponsorship by the Lutheran Immigration and Refugee Service. LIRS paid for my move from India to New York City where I lived in a small apartment for another few months. Although I was happy to be in America, I felt so alone in the great city of New York. I attended a large cathedral, but could not make friends easily. As soon as I told them I was from Iran, they assumed I was Muslim or a terrorist. Ever since the September 11th attack, New Yorkers are nervous about terrorists.

My wonderful parents knew where I was, but there was little they could do to help me. They wrote to a family friend, Hassid Al-Akkbah, who had left Iran six years earlier and now lived in Weston, Indiana, near Chicago. Hassid was kind enough to invite me to come and live with him temporarily. The Lutheran refugee organization agreed to pay for my move to Indiana, and asked the Trinity Lutheran Church in Weston to be my new sponsor.

Now that I am here in Weston, I am much happier. There is a committee of people at Trinity called the Refugee Committee. They have made me feel most welcome. They even helped me get a job at Barnes and Noble, a bookstore in Weston. My new friends include Mrs. Walker, the pastor's wife; Darrel Thomas; Mike Greenwood, a quiet bachelor; Reiner Holtz, who is from Germany; and a sweet little woman named Maria Olivera from Mexico. I call her my adopted grandma! She bakes cookies for me all the time! I do miss my mother and father in Tehran.

I like both the pastors at Trinity. Pastor Walker is a good Bible study leader and preacher. He says my English has improved in my first year here in the United States. The Assistant Pastor is a woman, Barbara Lambert. She is so big, and so funny. She makes me laugh. In the Muslim faith, a woman would never be allowed to speak in the mosque, or teach the scriptures. Pastor Barbara led an outstanding class on the prophets of the Old Testament, and I learned so much from her.

My roommate Hassid was very kind to let me live with him. He invited me to the mosque in Chicago, but I told him I am a Christian now. I told him how I had come to know Jesus while I was at the university in Tehran. He did not seem pleased. I hope to be able to afford my own apartment in a few more months.

Trinity Lutheran Church was beautiful at Christmas! They have a fine choir that sings magnificent Christian music. A large Christmas tree with white lights filled the chancel. The only thing I don't like here is how cold it gets. There are no mountains in Indiana, but there is plenty of snow. Last winter it stayed on the ground for several months. In the streets and parking lots, it got black and dirty. People say I should get used to it. I like America. I am most thankful to Allah, our heavenly Father, and to Jesus, and to the Lutherans for bringing me to America.

33

Pastor Barbara Lambert <small>was</small>
making friends quickly at Trinity. She and the music director, Sheila
Gordon, usually sat together at coffee hour. Their laughter could be heard
throughout the social hall. They were often joined by Jeannette, Trinity's
secretary, who was about the same age as Barbara. Jeannette was
extremely thin; some members privately thought she might be *anorexic*.
Barbara, who was extremely large, was accustomed to making jokes
about her own weight. She liked to ask Jeannette if she wanted to borrow
fifty or a hundred pounds!

After Sunday worship, folks moved downstairs for coffee and cookies. Mike
Greenwood spoke for a few minutes in the hallway with Omar Shufti. Mike
decided to have a cup of coffee before heading to Lucky's. His friends
there would still be moaning about the Colts. Their NFL season had ended
on February 7th with a disappointing loss. They were beaten by the New
Orleans Saints in Super Bowl XLIV, 31-17.

As he moved into the social hall, he spied Jeannette sitting at her usual
table with several friends. He picked up a cup of coffee and headed in
her direction. Jeannette was one of the few women Mike felt comfortable
around. He knew she was a lesbian and had a partner, and he figured there
was no danger that anyone would gossip about a relationship between
them. At Jeannette's table he recognized Pastor Barbara, but not the other
woman with her back to him, or the teenage girl to her left.

"May I join you?" he asked Barbara.

"Sure, have a seat," the pastor replied.

Mike pulled out a chair as Barbara said, "Have you met Jeannette's partner Kat?" Members at Trinity knew Jeannette had a partner; but many, including Mike, had not yet met her.

Kat turned to look up at the man about to sit next to her and stared in astonishment. Mike was equally shocked. "K . . . K . . . Kathy?" he stammered breathlessly.

"Mike? Oh my God! I haven't seen you in ages!"

"Apparently you two have met before!" Barbara commented, observing the startled interaction.

"Oh my God!" Kat said again, incredulous, shaking her head, as Mike took a seat. Autumn, a curious fifteen year old, leaned around her mother to see this man who had surprised her mother.

"You're Jeannette's partner?" Mike asked in amazement.

Kat smiled, "Yup. Eight years already."

"I can't believe it!" Mike sat shaking his head. He knew Jeannette had a partner named Kat, but Kat was Kathy! As he thought about his painful break-up with Kathy, not once, but twice, an embarrassing question came to mind. Mike leaned close to Kat's ear and whispered, "I don't know quite how to ask this, but . . . have you always been a . . . you know . . . a lesbian?"

"No, no . . . at least I don't think so," Kat whispered back, "or I didn't know I was." Everyone at the table was quiet, trying to look at each other so it didn't look like they were eavesdropping on the whispered conversation. Kat drew back and said, loudly enough for even Autumn to hear, "In high school . . . didn't I always say you were cute?"

Mike blushed. "Yeah . . . I guess."

"You knew Mike in high school?" Jeannette asked. Barbara and Autumn stared in amazement.

"Yup . . . we even went together for a little while," Kat answered, staring at Mike.

Mike was getting more and more embarrassed. He had been planning to enjoy a leisurely cup of coffee. Suddenly he felt overcome with conflicting emotions. "I think I'd better go. A friend of mine is waiting for me."

"Don't rush off, Mike," Barbara urged. "You haven't even finished your coffee yet."

"Yeah, but my friend's waiting," Mike insisted. He pushed his chair back, almost tripping on it as he stood up. "Excuse me, ladies; it's been a pleasure." Mike wasn't telling the truth exactly, but it seemed like a polite thing to say as he left. The women all watched him as Mike headed up the stairs for the parking lot.

Pastor Barbara couldn't contain her curiosity. "That was an interesting exchange," she said to Kat. "Want to tell us more?"

Kat giggled devilishly, "I'll bet Jeannette would like to hear more too! Right, Jeannette?"

"You went with Mike Greenwood in high school?" Jeannette responded. "Do tell us more."

Autumn, full of anticipation, begged, "Yeah, Mom, tell us more!" She was eager to learn more about her mom and another high school boyfriend, not the one who was her dad. She had heard more than enough about Kevin, the quarterback.

"Well," Kat continued, "Jeannette knows about Kevin Gianopolis, Autumn's dad. But I've never told anyone about Michael. I forgot that he attended this church too. I dated him my junior year, before I started going out with Kevin." All the women leaned over the table anxious to hear the story of Kat's high school romance. "Michael was *so* serious." Kat smiled as she remembered tousling Michael's curly hair. "I think he really loved me. It's just that I wasn't ready to get as serious as he was. Then along came Kevin." For the next few minutes Kat shared the story of her high school years, including a short version of the disaster with Kevin.

"Now that I think back, there was a second time I hooked up with Michael a few years later, after divorcing Kevin. In fact we met again, right here at Trinity, after a worship service. Autumn was in the nursery. We hung out with each other for another year or so and had a pretty good time."

"Oh, *that* Mike!" interrupted Autumn. "I remember him! I liked him! He was fun! How old was I, Mom, four or five?"

"Yes, just five, I think. Mike was nice enough, but I just couldn't make a commitment. A year later, along came Jeannette." Kat looked into Jeannette's eyes and smiled lovingly.

"I've liked Mike since I started working at Trinity," Jeannette commented. "Sounds like you gave Mike a pretty bad time, Kat. No wonder he tells everyone he's a confirmed bachelor."

"I've become better acquainted with Mike since he's been on the Refugee Committee," Pastor Barbara added. "I really like him, and now it makes sense to me why he never goes out with anyone."

"I certainly hope my coming here won't scare him away," Kat replied.

"Oh, I don't think so," Barbara responded. "Mike's been a member here quite a few years. He's a creature of habit. He'll be back."

"I hope so," Kat said, nodding thoughtfully.

"Me too!" Autumn added her two cents. "How exciting is this!?"

Mike drove to Lucky's Tavern, his mind racing. He could hardly wait to tell Charlie about what happened after church. When he stepped inside the dim room he saw Charlie at his usual place at the bar. Ron and Eddie were nowhere to be seen. Whitey began pouring a beer from the tap. "Hey, Charlie, you won't believe who I ran into at the church coffee hour today."

"Well, I haven't got the slightest idea . . . so, tell me."

Mike took his place on one of the old red vinyl bar stools. Whitey put the beer down in front of Mike. "Kathy . . . Kathy Stiletto. Except now she goes by Kat . . . . And you won't believe what else I learned."

"Isn't she the old girlfriend you told me about? The one who dumped you?"

"That's the one. But here's the latest news. Kat is a lesbian!"

"No! Your old girlfriend?"

"Yeah. And not only that, but she's married to our church secretary, Jeannette!"

"Holy crap!" Charlie shouted in amazement.

"You're tellin' me! I went to have coffee after worship . . . and Kat and Jeannette are sitting at the same table with Pastor Barbara. Kat's daughter Autumn was sitting with them; she's a teenager already!" Mike said breathlessly.

"Do you suppose her bein' a lesbian is why her marriage didn't work out? And maybe why she wouldn't marry you when you proposed?" Charlie asked.

"How the hell would I know?" Mike answered. "By the way, where's Eddie and Ron?"

"How the hell would I know?" Charlie repeated.

In the months that followed, Mike accepted the fact that Kat was a lesbian, and Kat was with Jeannette. He became more and more comfortable in their presence. He looked forward to his little coffee group after worship.

Jim Bornzin

One Sunday morning Jeannette said something to Pastor Barbara that started both of them giggling. It reminded him of his "sisters" when he was growing up. He smiled as he remembered the two little girls who lived with Jack and Charlotte. He remembered how they always had sisterly secrets; and how they giggled together, even though they weren't really sisters. They weren't related by blood; and yet, as far as they were concerned, they were *real sisters*.

One day when Pastor Paul was speaking about the Trinity church family, Mike thought about Barbara, Jeannette, Kat, and Autumn. They were like his sisters, not blood-related, but they felt like "real sisters."

34

Mike had gotten into a new habit at church. When he first began worshipping at Trinity, he would head right over to Lucky's as soon as church was over, but lately he had been staying for the coffee hour. He usually sat at the table with Pastor Barbara, Sheila Gordon, Jeannette, Kat and Autumn. Sometimes Pastor Paul would join them. The women were full of stories, and always laughing.

One Sunday morning Kat said, "Mike, why don't you join us for Autumn's volleyball game on Saturday? She's the star player on the Weston Warriors girls' team."

Mike hated to give up his afternoon at Lucky's, but replied, "Sure, why not. What time's the game?"

"Three o'clock," she answered, "See you at the gym."

Autumn had grown like a weed in high school. She was 6'-1" and very athletic. She was an outstanding swimmer, but preferred playing volleyball, her favorite sport. She inherited the athleticism from her dad, Kevin Gianopolis, whose name could still be found on an old brass cup in the Weston High School football trophy case.

On Saturday the gym was noisy, as it always was for Weston's home games. Mike climbed into the bleachers and sat down next to Kat and Jeannette. "Glad you could make it!" Jeannette hollered above the noise. The game had just started. Their old rivals from East Chicago took an early lead, 4-0. But Weston got into a rhythm and pretty soon it was tied. After several exchanges of serve, it was set point with Weston up 14-9. Autumn was really fired up. She served a line drive just over the net and down the line. The Mustangs thought it was going out of bounds, so they let it go . . . and it hit the line! First set of the match to the Warriors!

The match was two out of three. The second game started with Weston taking the early lead, 6-2. But East Chicago fought back and closed the score to within one point, 13-12. Weston scored again to make it 14-12. The crowd was going crazy! Mike felt like he was in high school again. Kathy Stiletto was yelling next to him. Oh, those were the days! The next serve led to a long, back and forth battle, with some fantastic digs by both teams. Finally, one of the Warriors put up a high set at the net for Autumn. Autumn jumped and spiked the ball hard between two Mustangs for the win. Warrior fans jumped from their seats! Yelling! Screaming! Mike jumped up, pumped his fist in the air, and yelled, "Way to go! Autumn! Hoo! Hoo! Autumn! Autumn!"

When he sat back down on the bench, Kat turned toward him, raised her arm, reached over and tousled his hair. "Hey, Michael! You're cute!" Mike's heart skipped a beat. How many years ago had she done that to him? Twenty? Twenty-five?

Kat was staring at him. She reached over again and put her hand over his ear, and rubbed the side of Mike's head with her thumb. Jeannette was watching. "Michael, I always loved your thick, wavy brown hair . . . but I DO BELIEVE the temples are getting gray!"

Kat laughed. Jeannette laughed. Mike blushed. Ol' Stiletto still had the touch.

*   *   *

Mike's promotion was no surprise to anyone. He had been at the Napa Auto Parts store longer than any other employee. He was well-liked by his fellow workers and they were very happy for him. The word soon spread to the church, and Pastor Barbara Lambert began planning a surprise for

Mike. She asked Jeannette to put a special announcement in the Sunday bulletin and in the newsletter. It read:

Congratulations to MIKE GREENWOOD!
On his recent promotion to MANAGER of Napa Auto Parts

In the bulletin, Jeannette added: Please stay for the coffee hour reception in honor of Mike.

On Sunday morning, Mike was surprised, embarrassed, and pleased to receive so much attention. He came into the coffee hour to find a cake decorated in NAPA colors, yellow and blue. Trinity members, led by the choir director, Sheila, burst into singing, "Congratulations to you! Congratulations to you! Congratulations Mike Greenwood! Congratulations to you!"

Mike was relieved that he didn't have to blow out candles—there weren't any—or cut the cake. Maybelle Stewart and Tillie Holtz cut and served the cake, insisting that Mike take the first big piece.

As Mike finished his last bite of the delicious NAPA cake, Jeannette leaned over his shoulder, and in a quiet voice said, "Did you know that Pastor Barbara planned this whole affair? I think she'd appreciate a big thank you."

Mike swallowed his last few drops of coffee and rose from his chair. Barbara was standing near the door saying good-by to one of the members. Mike approached her and Barbara turned. "I understand you're the one who put all of this surprise together," Mike said, smiling.

"Guilty as charged," Barbara replied.

"I just want to say thank you so much." Mike reached out to give her a hug.

Barbara moved forward. "I had fun doing it. Congratulations!"

As the two embraced, Mike noticed he couldn't wrap his arms completely around Barbara because of her size. He also noticed how warm and soft, yet strong, her arms felt around him. "Thanks again," Mike said.

35

Sunrise, sunset, *swiftly flow the years, one season following another, laden with happiness and tears.* Paul had always loved this song from *Fiddler on the Roof.* It described perfectly his experience at Trinity. The years had flown so swiftly since Paul and Cheri had interviewed in Weston, so long ago. Chip and Randy were little tykes then. And there certainly had been his share of happiness and tears.

At the November council meeting Paul reminded everyone that next year would be the 100th anniversary for Trinity. The signing of the church charter had occurred in September, giving them nine or ten months to plan and prepare for the Centennial. Fred Wilson, who was back on the council, suggested that a steering committee be formed. Paul agreed to prepare an article for the congregation's newsletter asking for volunteers and ideas for the 100 year celebration. Pastor Barbara wanted to work on hospitality. Paul said he was interested in putting together a booklet on Trinity's history.

By the following summer the steering committee had grown to fourteen people, with representatives from a dozen "task forces." Invitations were sent to former members and pastors. Jeannette worked additional hours in the office gathering addresses, keeping track of events for the celebration, and mailing special invitations and announcements.

A small "history task force" was gathering photos and artifacts from the distant past, trying to identify members in the old photos, planning how their history and memorabilia would be displayed, and preparing a booklet for distribution to members and the community.

Many of the long-term members were excited to hear that Pastor and Mrs. Bjornstad, who were now in their eighties, would be flying up from Florida for the Centennial week. Fred Schmidt agreed to pick them up at O'Hare Airport. Elmer Johannsen, who because of his poor eyesight, wasn't driving anymore, begged to ride along.

It was decided that the Centennial celebration would last eight days. Kickoff was an open house on Saturday, September 15. The church would be open from noon until 8 p.m. for people to walk through the display of Trinity's history. A devotional prayer service was scheduled for 7 p.m. at which guests and community visitors would be introduced and welcomed. Dessert would be served at 7:30 in the fellowship hall.

The official incorporation and signing of the church constitution by charter members would be celebrated on Sunday morning. A high service of Holy Communion was planned at which the bishop of the synod would preach and preside. Pastor Bjornstad, retired for many years, was thrilled to be asked to assist with communion distribution. The church would be open to visitors throughout the following week, and a closing service of thanksgiving would wrap up the Centennial the next Sunday.

Paul and Cheri were becoming more and more excited as September drew near. They were a little disappointed to learn that neither Chip nor Randy would be coming home for the celebration. Randy said he might drive back from Des Moines for one of the weekends, but couldn't be away from work for any longer. Chip and Linda said they were both too busy with work in California, but they would fly home for Christmas.

After months of preparation the Centennial week arrived. The entire church staff was exhausted by the planning, but energized enough by adrenalin to enjoy the opening service on Saturday night. The candlelight service was brief and beautiful, and the desserts served by the women were spectacular. Paul was pleased to see Pastor Carl and Donna Webster from the United Methodist Church, Father Scott Muldoon from St. Mary's, even Rabbi Isaac Chevitz from the synagogue. There were many people Paul didn't recognize, some were friends of members, some friends of Cheri's from the library, and others were visitors from the neighborhood. As the worshippers filed out, Paul was honored to shake hands with his detective friend, Sean Asplund, and Cheri's former boss, Miguel Juarez. When Paul and Cheri finally left the church, they stood together in the parking lot gazing up at the steeple. The cross was brightly lit.

At home they lit some logs in the fireplace, and then sat in their living room talking about the wonderful efforts put forth by so many members to make the celebration a success. Trinity Lutheran Church had truly become their extended family, one small branch of the family of God.

"Darrel Thomas has been such a blessing," Paul commented to Cheri, "not only to Reiner, but to me as well. We have Darrel to thank for the new cross and new lights on the steeple; Darrel to thank for leading the immigration committee and welcoming the Arriagas, and Omar Shufti. And speaking of Reiner Holtz, he and Tillie have become a real blessing too. Did you see Reiner ushering tonight?"

"Yes, I did," Cheri answered, "and Tillie was serving desserts in the kitchen with Maybelle Stewart. Remember how nervous both of them were when they first joined Trinity? I think Tillie is more relaxed than I've ever seen her. I think she's having fun!"

"Our lives have been so blessed by leaders like Fred Wilson and Howard Bardwell and Bill Trogdon," Paul continued.

"And don't forget wonderful treasurers like Liz Sterling!" Cheri said, grinning.

"Oh yes, Liz Sterling. What a chapter that was in our history!"

"And you've been blessed with two really great assistants in the office, Carol Van Schoyck and Jeannette Brownlee."

"And a delightful Assistant Pastor!" Paul added. "I think Barbara and I have been working really well together. She's been a real blessing to Trinity."

"She certainly brightens things up with her infectious laugh. Aren't she and Sheila a scream!"

Jim Bornzin

Cheri and Paul continued reminiscing and giving thanks for the next hour or two; they lost track of time. In prayer and conversation they gave thanks for all the saints, those who share the limelight with Paul, and those who work so humbly behind the scenes.

"We'd better get to bed," Paul announced. "I'm really tired, and I have to look somewhat alert tomorrow morning when the bishop shows up."

*   *   *

The Centennial Service of Holy Communion was all that Paul had hoped it would be. It began with a special tolling of the steeple bell. Chuck Kushman, who had been head usher for as long as anyone could remember, was given the honor of tolling the bell one hundred times before worship. He began five minutes prior to the start of the service. Four minutes later, plus or minus a few seconds, he pulled the rope for the one hundredth time. To everyone in the church and in the neighborhood, it seemed like it tolled forever. There were two calls to 9-1-1 asking if there was an emergency.

The church was filled with worshippers. The pews were packed uncomfortably tight. Twenty or thirty people stood in the side aisles and at the back of the sanctuary. Ushers scrambled to find folding chairs for everyone. The procession was led by a crucifer, the acolytes, and the choir. Behind the choir were the Lutheran clergy from Gary and East Chicago, and two of Trinity's former pastors. They were followed by Pastor Barbara Lambert, Pastor Paul Walker, and Bishop Troy Pierson.

The bishop's message was affirming and full of hope for the next hundred years. The choir anthem accompanied by organ and trumpet was as stirring as anything Sheila had ever conducted. At the time for communion, Pastor Walker, Pastor Lambert, and Pastor Bjornstad came up to the altar. The bishop handed Barbara a plate of communion wafers. He gave Paul two chalices—one with wine, one with grape juice. Pastor Bjornstad also had two chalices. They took positions on the floor of the nave, in front of the chancel entrance. Worshippers had been instructed on intinction: come forward up the center aisle, receive the wafer, dip it into the wine or grape juice, and return to your seat using the side aisles.

Pastor Bjornstad stood in the chancel looking confused. He had always served members communion at the rail. Apparently he had not heard the directions given by the bishop. Barbara turned around, stepped up into the chancel, took the elderly pastor by the arm and gently led him to the front of the chancel and down the two steps. From that point on, all went smoothly.

At the conclusion of worship Paul invited everyone to tour the building to see the historical displays in each room, and come to the fellowship hall downstairs for coffee and cake. The steering committee had discussed a potluck and decided against a sit-down dinner because there simply would not be enough room in the fellowship hall.

The Centennial Cake was a masterpiece; four tiers high with large numerals **100** at the very top. The three cakes which formed the bottom tier each had the words 𝕿𝖗𝖎𝖓𝖎𝖙𝖞 𝕷𝖚𝖙𝖍𝖊𝖗𝖆𝖓 in Old English gold frosting. Coffee, tea, and punch were served as quickly as possible as the line of people came down the stairs.

Paul and Cheri and Troy, the bishop, were among the last to come into the hall. They had been busy visiting in the sanctuary with so many people after worship. Across the room they heard the sound of raucous laughter. Jeannette, Sheila, Barbara, Mike, Kat and Autumn were sharing favorites from *The Princess Bride*.

"My favorite," said Mike, "was the Sicilian pirate who kidnapped the princess. Every time he was foiled by Sir Farm-boy, he would shout, INCONCEIVABLE!"

"Inconceivable!" mimicked Autumn. "I have a school friend who uses that all the time."

"And this one," Mike continued. "My name is Inigo Montoya. You killed my father. Prepare to die!" Everyone at the table roared with laughter at Mike's imitation.

"I loved the old sorcerer," stated Barbara as she stood up and leaned over Mike, examining his head. "He's not *completely* dead. He's just *mostly* dead!" The table erupted again.

Mike finished his coffee and stood to leave. "Oh, Mike," Barbara interrupted his departure. "Before you go, would you fetch me a fresh cup of coffee?"

Mike bowed deeply. "As you wish . . . ." And again, everyone laughed loudly.

Mike returned a few moments later with a cup of hot coffee for Barbara, bowed, and announced, "I am expected at Lucky's. By your leave!"

"Go! Get out of here!" Kat dismissed him with a wave of her hand.

Paul, Cheri, and Troy had cake and coffee in hand as they found a place at an empty table. "Those crazy nuts!" Paul said to the bishop. "They're like a bunch of kids!"

"God's kids," Troy responded, "children of God having fun. I think it's great to hear laughter in church."

"So do I," said Cheri.

Paul nodded in agreement and offered a silent prayer before digging into the cake. *Heavenly Father, thank you for the privilege of being your children. You have blessed us in so many ways. Trinity Lutheran is truly a family of God. Help us to continue extending your love to all families of the world, through your most special Son, Jesus Christ, our Savior. Amen.*

36

Charlie, Ron and Eddie were waiting at Lucky's Tavern when Mike arrived. "Well, look what the cat dragged in," Ron drawled as Mike approached the table.

"How was church today?" Charlie asked.

"Good, good . . . big crowd . . . hundredth anniversary . . ." Mike said as he pulled out a chair and sat down. "What's on?" he asked, looking up toward the big-screen TV.

"Golf tournament," Eddie answered. "Colts aren't playing today. No racing either. So I guess we watch golf."

Whitey came to the table with a beer for Mike. "Anybody need a refill yet?" They shook their heads no. "Holler when you're hungry," Whitey said as he turned back toward the bar.

"How's the arthritis, Eddie?" Mike asked.

"Not too bad right now," Eddie replied. "Doctor gave me a shot in my knee about a week ago, and since then it hasn't hurt much at all."

The four of them chatted intermittently for about fifteen minutes. The door of the tavern opened and two women walked in. The bright light from outside made it impossible to see who they were at first. The women were also having trouble seeing as their eyes adjusted to the dim light inside. They walked toward the bar.

Jim Bornzin

"What can I get for you ladies?" Whitey asked.

"We're looking for Mike Greenwood," one of the women said. The men at the table all looked at Mike.

"He's right over there," Whitey said, pointing toward the table.

Mike recognized them as soon as they turned toward him; it was Jeannette and Kat. Mike stood up as they approached the table. "Hi, Jeannette! Hi, Kat! I'd like you to meet my friends. This is Charlie. This is Eddie. And that's Ron." They exchanged *How-do-you-do's* and *Nice-to-meet-you's*.

"Mike, we'd like to talk to you," Jeannette said, and then added, "privately."

"Sure, sure. Want to sit back there in the corner booth?" Mike asked, gesturing to the rear of the tavern.

"That'll be okay," Kat said. They took their seats in the booth. The television was loud enough that neither group could hear the other's conversation.

"Hey, guys, do you know who that is?" Charlie whispered to his friends.

"No, I've never seen them before," Ron replied.

"The shorter one, the one with the short blond hair? That's Kat, Kathy Stiletto, the girl Mike dated in high school," Charlie informed them.

"Do you suppose she's come to ask him for a date?" Eddie joked.

"Naw, not a chance," Charlie answered. "Mike told me she's a lesbian now. And the other woman is the secretary from Mike's church. She's Kat's partner."

"Looks like they're havin' a real serious discussion," Ron observed.

Kat, Jeannette, and Mike were indeed having a very serious discussion. "Mike . . . Jeannette and I have been talking since church this morning about you and Barbara." Kat was looking deep into Mike's eyes.

Mike was uncomfortable hearing his name paired with the pastor's. "What about me and Barbara?" he asked defensively.

Jeannette spoke next. "You know I work in the office with Barbara and we've become fairly close."

"Yeah," Mike responded, anxious about what was coming.

"Well, I was telling Kat about some of the things I've heard Barbara say about you." Jeannette hesitated. "Actually, it's not just *what* she says, it's more the *way* she says it."

"I don't get the drift," Mike said with a puzzled frown.

Kat interrupted, "Look, Mike, what Jeannette is trying to say is that Barbara really likes you a lot . . . . I mean . . . a lot."

Mike was beginning to guess where this was leading, and it made him even more uncomfortable. "I like Pastor Barbara a lot . . . but that doesn't mean . . . that doesn't mean there's anything *between us* . . . if you know what I mean."

"Don't misunderstand," Jeannette responded, "we're not suggesting anything has happened between you. In fact, it's just the opposite. Kat and I were saying that as far as you're concerned, there is absolutely nothing between you and Pastor Barbara."

"I think what Jeannette is saying is maybe you should think about Barbara . . . as a woman . . . not just as a pastor."

Mike suddenly remembered the hug Barbara had given him at a coffee hour not long ago. And just as quickly, he dismissed the memory. "Okay, okay, I like Barbara as a woman . . . as a friend. But I'm a confirmed bachelor, remember? I'm not interested in a relationship; I'm too old; I'm too set in my ways."

Both women smiled. Jeannette spoke again, "Funny . . . that's exactly what I've heard Barbara say about herself. She's not interested in men; she's too old; she's too set in her ways."

"Mike," Kat reached over the table and put her hand on Mike's arm. "You and Barbara were having such a great time at coffee hour this morning, doing your lines from *The Princess Bride*."

"Yeah, that was fun! Barbara cracked me up with her line, 'He's not *completely* dead; he's just *mostly* dead.'"

"Do you think she might have meant YOU?" Kat asked.

Mike was stunned. *Me? Dead? Not dead; just mostly dead.*

"Remember when Barbara asked you to refill her coffee cup?" Jeannette asked.

"And you said, 'As you wish' . . ." Kat added, looking again into Mike's eyes.

Mike squirmed, and pulled his arm away from Kat's touch. "Yeah, but that was just a line from the movie."

"Was it?" Kat asked.

Mike remembered that in the movie, the princess finally realized . . . "*As you wish*" really meant "I love you." Mike was looking at Kat but thinking about Barbara, wondering if he could possibly have those giddy feelings again.

Jeannette and Kat looked at each other and wondered if they had finally gotten their message across. They weren't trying to be match-makers. Jeannette was confident she knew how Barbara was already feeling about Mike. She just wanted Mike to be aware of how Barbara felt toward him.

She also wanted Mike to be aware of his own feelings, and his defenses . . . how guarded he was of his feelings.

After what seemed like an eternity of silence, Jeannette spoke once more, "I think Barbara is wishing you'd ask her out . . . for a nice dinner . . . and . . . maybe a movie."

Mike considered the idea. *Jeannette and Kat weren't playing games. They simply wanted him to know about Barbara's feelings toward him. A date with a pastor? Not a date exactly . . . just a pleasant evening with a friend . . . a really nice, intelligent, reliable woman . . . who could also be a lot of fun.*

"Well, I might . . ." Mike said, beginning to feel a glimmer of excitement. "I just might do that."

ABOUT THE AUTHOR

Jim Bornzin is an ordained Lutheran pastor, married and living in Silverton, Oregon. During forty years of ordained ministry, he served six congregations in Oregon, Washington, and Illinois. Jim has also served as a hospital chaplain in Spokane, Washington and Silverton, Oregon, and as a volunteer police chaplain in Coos Bay, Oregon. Jim is deeply committed to ecumenism and a deeper understanding of all religions. All of these experiences have influenced his second novel *Tales from Trinity*.

He has worked with numerous community agencies, both as a volunteer and board member. These include: Habitat for Humanity, Helpline Information and Referral, Temporary Help in Emergency House, and Rockford Area Lutheran Ministries. As a parish pastor, Jim appreciated forming deep and lasting relationships with church members, often walking with them through crisis situations.

Jim Bornzin

Jim received his bachelor's degree in Science Engineering from Northwestern University. Working several summers in various engineering departments convinced him that he should seek a career in something more people-oriented. His theological education includes a Master of Divinity, a Master of Sacred Theology from the Lutheran School of Theology at Chicago, and three quarters of Clinical Pastoral Education at Deaconess Hospital in Spokane. He was ordained in 1967. For more of Jim's creativity visit: *jimbornzin.com*